W9-BYO-424

ICEBERG

Now available for the first time
in an Archway edition.

DIRK PITT®

He is a man of action who lives by the moment and
for the moment . . . without regret. A graduate of the
Air Force Academy, son of a United States Senator,
and Special Projects director for the U.S. National
Underwater & Marine Agency (NUMA), he is cool,
courageous and resourceful—a man of complete
honor at all times and of absolute ruthlessness when-
ever necessary.

Books by Clive Cussler

ICEBERG
INCA GOLD
SHOCK WAVE

Available from Archway Paperbacks
Published by Pocket Books

For orders other than by individual consumers, Pocket Books grants a discount on the purchase of **10 or more** copies of single titles for special markets or premium use. For further details, please write to the Vice President of Special Markets, Pocket Books, 1230 Avenue of the Americas, 9th Floor, New York, NY 10020-1586.

For information on how individual consumers can place orders, please write to Mail Order Department, Simon & Schuster Inc., 100 Front Street, Riverside, NJ 08075.

Iceberg

A DIRK PITT® ADVENTURE

AN ARCHWAY PAPERBACK
Published by POCKET BOOKS
New York   London   Toronto   Sydney   Singapore

The sale of this book without its cover is unauthorized. If you purchased this book without a cover, you should be aware that it was reported to the publisher as "unsold and destroyed." Neither the author nor the publisher has received payment for the sale of this "stripped book."

This book is a work of fiction. Names, characters, places and incidents are products of the author's imagination or are used fictiously. Any resemblance to actual events or locales or persons, living or dead, is entirely coincidental.

An Archway Paperback published by
POCKET BOOKS, a division of Simon & Schuster Inc.
1230 Avenue of the Americas, New York, NY 10020

Copyright © 1975 by Clive Cussler
Abridged Archway Paperback Edition copyright © 2000 by
Clive Cussler

Unabridged version published in paperback in 1986 by
Pocket Books

All rights reserved, including the right to reproduce this book or portions thereof in any form whatsoever. For information address Pocket Books, 1230 Avenue of the Americas, New York, NY 10020

ISBN: 0-671-78626-1

First Archway Paperback printing August 2000

10 9 8 7 6 5 4 3 2 1

AN ARCHWAY PAPERBACK and colophon are registered trademarks of Simon & Schuster Inc.

DIRK PITT is a registered trademark of Clive Cussler.

Front cover illustration by Franco Accornero

Printed in the U.S.A.

IL 6+

Iceberg

Prologue

The girl began the agonizing struggle back to consciousness. A dim and hazy light greeted her slowly opening eyes while a disgusting stench invaded her nostrils. Then suddenly, before she had a chance to fight the panic mushrooming inside her, the yellow slime on the floor rose. Terrified beyond all reason, she began screaming—screaming insanely as the abomination crawled ever upward. And then, just as the unspeakable horror touched the girl's lips, a vibrating roar and a phantom, unseen voice echoed throughout the darkened chamber.

"Sorry to interrupt your study period, Lieutenant, but duty calls."

Lieutenant Sam Neth snapped the book in his hands shut. "Thanks a lot," he said to the sour-faced man seated beside him in the cockpit of the droning aircraft. "Every time I come to an interesting part, you butt in."

Ensign James Rapp nodded toward the book, its paperback cover illustrating a girl struggling in a pool of yellow slime. "How can you read that garbage?"

"Garbage?" Neth grimaced painfully. "Not only do you invade my privacy, Ensign, you also think of yourself as my personal literary critic!" He sighed, then straightened up in his seat and peered through the windshield at the sea below.

The United States Coast Guard patrol plane was four hours, twenty minutes into a routine eight-hour iceberg surveillance and charting mission. Visibility was diamond-clear under a cloudless sky, and the wind barely moved the rolling swells—a unique condition for the North Atlantic in the middle of March.

In the cockpit, Neth, with four of the crew members, piloted and navigated the huge four-engined Boeing aircraft, while the other six crewmen took up office in the cargo section, eyeballing the radar scopes and other scientific instruments. Neth checked his watch and then turned the plane on a sweeping arc, settling the nose on a straight course toward the Newfoundland coast.

Back in the dimly lighted belly of the plane, Seaman First Class Buzz Hadley stared intently at the radar set, his face reflecting an unearthly green glow from the scope. "I have a weird reading, sir. Eighteen miles, bearing three-four-seven."

Neth flicked the mike switch. "Come, come, Hadley. What do you mean by *weird?* Are you reading an iceberg, or have you tuned your set into an old Dracula movie?"

"Maybe he's picking up your horror novel," Rapp grunted.

Hadley came back on. "Judging from the configuration and size, it's a berg, but my signal is much too strong for ordinary ice."

"Okay." Neth sighed. "We'll have a look-see." He fitted a battered pair of flying goggles to his eyes, braced himself for the blasting cold, and opened his side window for a closer look. "Here she is," he said, motioning to Rapp. "Make a couple of passes."

The icy air tore at Neth's skin until it turned numb. He gritted his teeth and kept his eyes glued to the berg. The huge ice mass looked like a ghostly clipper ship under full sail as it floated gracefully beneath the cockpit windows.

Rapp eased the throttles back and twisted the controls slightly, sending the patrol plane into a wide, sweeping bank to port. Three times he circled, waiting for a sign from Neth to level the plane out.

Finally, after what seemed an eternity to Rapp, Neth pulled his head back into the cabin, closed the side window, and pressed the mike switch. "Sloan? Did you see it?"

"I saw it." Lieutenant Jonis Sloan's voice came over the intercom. "I didn't think it was possible." Sloan was the chief ice observer aboard the patrol plane.

"Neither did I," Neth said, "but it's down there—a ship, a ghost ship inbedded in the ice."

Neth slipped off the goggles and raised the thumb of his right hand in the air, motioning up. Gratefully

Rapp sighed and leveled out the patrol plane, putting a comfortable margin of space between the aircraft's underbelly and the cold Atlantic.

"Excuse me, Lieutenant." Hadley came through over the headphones. He was hunched over his radar set, painstakingly studying a little white blip almost in the exact center of the scope. "For what it's worth, the overall length of that thing in the berg is in the neighborhood of one hundred and twenty-five feet."

"A derelict fishing trawler, most likely." Neth vigorously massaged his cheeks, wincing at the pain as the circulation began to return.

"Shall I contact District Headquarters in New York and request a rescue party?" Rapp asked.

Neth shook his head. "No need to rush a rescue ship. It's obvious there are no survivors. We'll make a detailed report after we've landed in Newfoundland."

There was a pause. Then Sloan's voice came through.

"Make a pass over the berg, skipper. I'll drop a dye marker on it for quick identification."

The Boeing, its four engines still turning at reduced power, swept over the stately iceberg. Back at the cargo door, Sloan raised his arm, pausing. Then at Neth's spoken command, Sloan tossed a gallon jar full of red dye out into space. The jar grew smaller and smaller, shrinking to a tiny speck before finally striking the smooth cliff face of the target. Peering back, Sloan could see a bright vermilion streak spreading slowly down the million-ton mound of ice.

"Right on the button." Neth said. "The search party won't have any trouble spotting that one." Then suddenly grim-faced, he stared down toward the spot where the unknown ship lay entombed. "I wonder if we'll ever know what happened to them?"

Rapp's eyes took on a thoughtful look. "They couldn't have asked for a bigger tombstone."

The cabin became clouded by a silence that seemed intensified by the drone of the plane's engines. Neither man spoke for several moments, each lost in his own thoughts. They could only look at the ominous pinnacle of white rising out of the sea and speculate on the enigma locked beneath its icy mantle.

When the Coast Guard patrol plane had disappeared and the last steady beat of its engines had faded away in the cold salt air as it headed for Newfoundland, the towering iceberg once again lay enshrouded in the deathly stillness it had endured since being broken from a glacier and forced into the sea off the west coast of Greenland nearly a year before.

Then suddenly there was a slight but perceptible movement on the ice just above the waterline of the berg. Two indistinct shapes slowly transformed into two men who rose to their feet and stared in the direction of the retreating aircraft. From more than twenty paces they would have been invisible to the unaided eye—both wore white snowsuits that blended in perfectly with the colorless background.

They stood there for a long time, patiently waiting and listening. When they were satisfied the patrol

plane was not returning, one of the men knelt and
brushed away the ice, revealing a small radio transmitter and receiver. Extending the ten-foot telescopic
aerial, he set the frequency and began turning the
crank handle. He didn't have to crank very hard or
very long. Someone, somewhere, was keeping a
tight watch on the same frequency, and the answer
came almost immediately.

CLIVE CUSSLER

1

"Sorry to drag you from sunny California, but this whole project has been dumped in our lap." Admiral James Sandecker, a small, fire-haired, griffon-faced man, and Chief Director of the National Underwater & Marine Agency, waved a seven-inch cigar in the air like a baton. "We're supposed to be engaged in scientific underwater research. Why us? Why not the Navy? You'd think the Coast Guard could handle its own problems." He shook his head in irritation, puffed on the cigar. "Anyway, we're stuck with it."

Air Force Major Dirk Pitt, Special Projects Director for NUMA, laid a yellow folder marked *confidential* on the admiral's desk. "I didn't think it was possible for a ship to freeze up in the middle of an iceberg."

"It's extremely unlikely, but Dr. Hunnewell assures me it could happen." Dr. Bill Hunnewell, Director of the California Institute of Oceanography and the world's leading authority on ice formations, was also assigned to the project.

"It's already been four days since the Coast Guard's sighting. That overgrown ice cube could have drifted halfway to the Azores by now," Pitt said.

"Dr. Hunnewell has charted the current and drift rate to within a thirty-square-mile area. If your vision is good, you shouldn't have any trouble spotting the berg, particularly since the Coast Guard dropped a red dye marker on it. I want you to land on the berg and investigate just what's inside that ship."

"This may come as a surprise, Admiral, but I've never set a copter down on an iceberg before."

"It's very possible no one else has either. That's why I requested you as my Special Projects Director." Sandecker smiled mischievously. "In fact, I wouldn't have it any other way."

Pitt shrugged helplessly. "I don't know why I always give in so easily to you, Admiral. I'm beginning to think you have me pegged as a first-class pigeon."

A broad grin rode across Sandecker's face. "You said it, not me."

Less than twenty-four hours later, Pitt and Hunnewell were flying the helicopter Ulysses north of the 15th parallel of latitude over the forty-degree waters of the North Atlantic.

"I don't like it," Hunnewell shouted above the racket of the helicopter's engine exhaust. "We should have sighted something by now."

Pitt looked at his watch. "Timewise, we're in good shape. Still over two hours of fuel to go."

"Can't you go higher? If we double our range of vision, we'd double our chances of detecting the iceberg."

Pitt shook his head. "No can do. We'd also double the possibility of our own detection. It's safer if we stay at a hundred and fifty feet."

"We must find it today," Hunnewell said, an anxious expression on his cherub face. "Tomorrow may be too late for a second try." He studied the chart draped across his knees for a moment then picked up a pair of binoculars and focused off to the north at several icebergs floating together in a cluster.

"Have you noticed any bergs that come close to matching the description we're looking for?" Pitt asked.

"We crossed one about an hour ago that passed the size and configuration requirements, but there was no red dye on its walls. Never since my high school trigonometry class have my calculations been so far off."

"Perhaps a change in wind direction blew the berg on a different course."

"Impossible," Hunnewell grunted. "An iceberg's underwater mass is seven times the size of what shows on the surface. Nothing but an ocean current has the slightest effect on its movement. It can easily move with the current against a twenty-knot wind."

"An irresistible force and an immovable object rolled up into one lump."

"That and much more—near indestructible." Hunnewell talked as he peered through the glasses. "Of course, they break up and melt soon after drifting south into warmer waters. But during their passage to the Gulf Stream, they bow neither to storm nor man. Glacier icebergs have been blasted by torpedoes, eight-inch naval guns, massive doses of thermite bombs, and tons of coal dust to soak up the sun and speed up the melting process. The results were comparable to the damage a herd of elephants might suffer after a slingshot bombardment by a tribe of anemic pygmies."

Pitt went into a steep bank, dodging around the sheer sides of a high-pinnacled berg—a maneuver that had Hunnewell clutching his stomach.

He checked the chart again. Two hundred square miles covered and nothing achieved. He said: "Let's try due north for fifteen minutes. Then head back east to the edge of the ice pack. Then south for ten minutes before we cut west again."

"One graduated box pattern to the north coming up," Pitt said. He tilted the controls slightly, holding the helicopter in a side-swinging movement until the compass read zero degrees.

The minutes wore on and multiplied and the fatigue began to show in the deepening lines around Hunnewell's eyes.

Pitt's voice broke the silence. "The red dye marker. Could be it washed away in the storm yesterday?"

"Fortunately no. The dye contains calcium chloride, a necessary ingredient for deep penetration—takes weeks, sometimes months for the stain to melt away."

"That leaves us with one other possibility."

"I know what you're thinking," Hunnewell said flatly. "And you can perish the thought. I've worked closely off and on with the Coast Guard for over thirty years, and I've never known them to mistake an ice position sighting."

"That's it then. A million-ton chunk of ice evaporated into—"

Pitt left the sentence unfinished, partly because the helicopter was beginning to drift off course, partly because he glimpsed something. Hunnewell suddenly stiffened in his seat and leaned forward, the binoculars jammed against his eye sockets.

"I have it," Hunnewell cried.

Pitt didn't wait for a command; he dipped the helicopter and headed toward the direction indicated by Hunnewell's binoculars. As they bore down on the great ice giant, Pitt and Hunnewell shared a strange sense of emptiness brought on by the eerie appearance of the mystery ship itself. Neither man had ever seen anything quite like it. The sight seemed so unreal that it was difficult for Pitt to accept the visible fact of its existence. As he adjusted the controls and lowered the helicopter to the ice, he half expected the entombed vessel to vanish.

Pitt tried to land on a smooth spot near the berg's edge, but the sloping angle of the ice proved too great; he finally put down directly on top of the derelict. Hunnewell leaped from the helicopter just before the skids kissed the ice, and had already paced the derelict from bow to stern when Pitt joined him.

"Odd," Hunnewell murmured, "most odd. Nothing protrudes above the surface, not even the masts and radar antenna. Every square inch is sealed solidly under the ice."

Pitt sniffed the air. "Smell anything out of the ordinary, Doc?"

Hunnewell tilted his head back and inhaled slowly. "There is something of an odor. Too faint though. I can't make it out."

"You don't travel in the right circles," Pitt said, grinning. "If you'd get out of your laboratory more often and learn a bit about life, you'd recognize the distinct aroma of burned garbage."

"Where's it coming from?"

Pitt nodded at the ship under his feet. "Where else but down there."

Hunnewell shook his head. "No way. It's a scientific fact, you can't smell an inorganic substance inside a block of ice from the outside."

"The old proboscis never lies." The midday warmth was beginning to overcome the cold, so Pitt unzipped his flight jacket. "There must be a leak in the ice."

"You and your educated nose," Hunnewell said acidly. "I suggest you stop playing bloodhound and start placing the thermite charges. The only way we're going to get inside the wreck is by melting the ice mantle."

"Dr. Hunnewell," Pitt said quietly, "I won't argue the fact that your name is known far and wide for your hyper-scientific intellect. However, like most superbrains, your mental depth for practical, every-day run-of-the-mill matters is sadly lacking. Thermite charges, ice picks, you say. Why bother with complex and muscle-exerting schemes when we can simply perform an open sesame routine?"

"You're standing on glacial ice," Hunnewell said. "It's hard and it's solid. You can't walk through it."

"Sorry, my friend, you're dead wrong," Pitt said.

Hunnewell eyed him suspiciously. "Prove it!"

"What I'm getting at is, the labor has already been done." He pointed dramatically upward. "Please observe."

Hunnewell lifted a quizzical eyebrow and looked upward and intently studied the broad face of the steep ice slope. Along the outer edges and near the lower base, only a few yards from where Pitt and Hunnewell stood, the ice was smooth and even. But beginning at the summit and working downward into the middle of the slope, the ice was as pockmarked as the moon.

"Well now," Hunnewell murmured, "it does appear that someone went to a lot of trouble to remove the Ice Patrol's red dye stain." He gave a long expressionless look at the towering ice pinnacle, then turned back to Pitt. "Why would someone chip the stain out by hand when they could have easily erased all trace with explosives?"

"I can't answer that," Pitt said. "Maybe they were afraid of cracking the berg, or maybe they didn't have explosives, who can say? However, I'll bet a month's salary that our clever little pals did more than merely chip ice. They most certainly found a way to enter the derelict."

"So all we do now is look for a flashing sign that says *enter here*." Hunnewell's tone was sarcastic. He wasn't used to being outguessed, and his expression showed that he didn't like it.

"A soft spot in the ice would be more appropriate."

"I suppose," Hunnewell said, "you're suggesting a camouflaged cover over some sort of ice tunnel."

"The thought had crossed my mind."

The doctor peered over the top of his glasses at Pitt. "Let's get on it then."

It shouldn't have been all that difficult, not by a long shot, yet it didn't go as easily as Pitt had figured. The unpredictable occurred when Hunnewell lost his footing on the slope and slid helplessly toward a steep ledge that dropped into the icy sea. He fell forward, desperately clawing at the ice, his nails scratching and bending painfully backward through the hard surface. He slowed momentarily, but not enough. His fall happened so abruptly that his ankles were already scraping the edge of the thirty-foot drop before he thought of shouting for help.

Pitt had been busily prying up a chunk of loose ice when he heard the cry. He swung around, took in Hunnewell's deteriorating plight, had a lightning impression of how impossible rescue would be once the doctor had fallen into the freezing water, and in one swift movement tore off his flight jacket and flung himself across the slope in a flying leap, feet first, legs lifted crazily in the air. Suddenly, with

only a leg's length remaining before he collided with
Hunnewell, Pitt brought his feet flashing down with
a power and swiftness that, even in these desperate
circumstances, made him grunt in pain as his heels
crashed through the ice, dug in tenaciously and
brought him to a muscle-jarring stop. Then, as if
triggered by instinct, in the same motion he threw a
sleeve of his jacket to Hunnewell.

The thoroughly frightened scientist needed no
coaxing. He grasped the nylon fabric with a grip that
no vise could have equaled and hung on, trembling
for almost a minute, waiting for his heart to slow
down to a few beats above normal. Fearfully, he
stole a glance sideways and saw what his numbed
senses could not feel—the edge of the ice ledge cut
across his waist at the navel.

"When you're up to it," Pitt said, his voice calm
but pierced with a noticeable trace of tenseness, "try
pulling yourself toward me."

Hunnewell shook his head. "I can't," he murmured hoarsely. "It's all I can do to hold on."

Pitt bent over between his outstretched legs and
tightened his grip on the jacket. "We're sitting here
through the courtesy of two hard rubber heels, not
steel cleats. It won't take much for the ice to crack
around them." He flashed an encouraging grin at
Hunnewell. "Make no sudden movement. I'm going
to pull you clear of the ledge."

Cautiously, an inch at a time, Pitt hauled Hunnewell slowly upward. It took him an agonizing
sixty seconds before he had Hunnewell's head on a

plane between his knees. Then Pitt, one hand at a time, let go of the jacket and grabbed Hunnewell under the armpits.

"That was the easy part," Pitt said. "The next exercise is up to you."

His hands free, Hunnewell wiped a sleeve across his sweaty brow. "I can't make any guarantees."

"Your dividers, are they on you?"

Hunnewell's expression went blank for a moment. Then he nodded. "Inside breast pocket."

"Good," Pitt murmured. "Now climb over me and stretch out full length. When your feet are solidly on my shoulders, take out the dividers and jam them into the ice."

"A piton!" Hunnewell exclaimed, suddenly aware. "Truly clever of you, Major."

Hunnewell began hauling himself over Pitt's prostrate form, straining like a locomotive climbing the Rockies, but he made it. Then, with Pitt's hands firmly clamped on his ankles, Hunnewell pulled out the steel-pointed dividers that he normally used for plotting distances on charts and rammed them deeply into the ice.

"Okay," Hunnewell grunted.

"Now we'll repeat the process," Pitt said. "Can you hold on?"

"Make it quick," Hunnewell answered. "My hands are nearly numb."

Tentatively, one heel still imbedded in the ice as a safety measure, Pitt tested his weight on Hunnewell's legs. The dividers gripped firm. Working as swiftly and as smoothly as a cat, Pitt crept past Hunnewell, felt his hands grope over the edge of the slope where it leveled out, and wiggled up onto safe ground. He didn't waste an instant. Almost immediately, it seemed to Hunnewell, Pitt was throwing down a nylon line from the helicopter. Half a minute later, the pale and exhausted oceanographer sat on the ice.

Pitt clapped Hunnewell on the shoulder and helped him to his feet. He stopped abruptly and said sharply: "Your hands look like you held them against a grindstone."

Hunnewell lifted his hands and stared indifferently at the bleeding fingers. "Not really as bad as they look. A bit of antiseptic and a manicure and they'll be as good as new."

"Come on," Pitt said. "There's a first-aid kit in the copter. I'll fix them up for you."

A few minutes later, as Pitt tied the last small bandage, Hunnewell asked, "Did you find any sign of a tunnel before I took my spill?"

"It's a slick piece of work," Pitt replied. "The entire circumference of the entrance cover is beveled, a perfect match with the surrounding ice. If someone hadn't gotten careless and cut a small handgrip, I'd have walked right over it."

Hunnewell flexed his fingers and solemnly studied the eight little bandages masking the tips. His eyes seemed strained and his face looked weary.

Pitt walked over and raised a round slab of ice three feet in diameter by three inches thick, revealing a crudely carved tunnel barely large enough for one man to crawl through. Instinctively he turned his head away—a powerful, acrid stench of burnt paint, fabric and fuel, mingled with torched metal, rose from the opening.

"That should prove I can detect smells through an ice cube," Pitt said.

"Yes, you've passed the nose test," Hunnewell said smugly. "But you've failed miserably on your thermite charge theory. That's nothing but a burned-out hulk down there." He paused to give Pitt a scholarly gaze over the tops of his spectacles. "We could have blasted until next summer without doing any damage to the derelict."

Pitt shrugged. "Win a few, lose a few." He passed a spare flashlight to Hunnewell. "I'll go first. Give me five minutes before you follow."

Hunnewell crouched at the edge of the ice tunnel as Pitt knelt to enter.

"Two. I'll give you two minutes, no more. Then I'll be right behind you."

The tube, illuminated by the shattered rays of the sun through the ice crystals above, ran downward at a thirty-degree angle for twenty feet, stopping at the blackened steel plates, charred and bent, of the hull. The smell by this time was so strong that Pitt found it an effort just to breathe. He shook off the irritating odor and dragged himself to within a foot of the fire-scarred metal, discovering that the tunnel curved and paralleled the hull for another ten feet, ending finally at an open hatch, savagely twisted and distorted. He could barely imagine the white-hot temperatures responsible.

Crawling over the jagged edge of the hatchway, he stood up and swung the beam of his flashlight, surveying the heat-defaced walls. It was impossible to tell what purpose the compartment served. Every square inch was gutted by the terrible intensity of the fire.

Pitt suddenly felt a dread of the unknown. He stood dead-still for several moments, forcing his mind to regain control of his emotions before he stepped across the debris toward the door leading to the alleyway and shone the light into the darkness beyond.

The beam touched the whole black length as far as the stairway to a lower deck. The corridor was barren except for the charred ashes of a carpet. It was the silence that was eerie. No creaking of the plates, no throb of the engines, no lapping of water against a weed-encrusted hull, nothing, only the complete soundlessness of a void. He hesitated in the doorway for a long minute; his first thought was that something had gone terribly, terribly wrong with Admiral Sandecker's plans. This wasn't what they had been led to expect at all.

Hunnewell came through the hatchway and joined him. He stood next to Pitt, staring at the blackened walls, the distorted and crystallized metal, and the melted hinges that once held a wooden door. Wearily he leaned against the doorway, his eyes half closed, shaking his head as if coming out of a trance.

They went out into the alleyway, stepping through the ashes and debris on the deck, moved to the next compartment, and entered. It had been the radio room. Most of the ruins were scarcely recognizable. The bunk and furniture were skeletons of charred wood, the remains of the radio equipment one congealed mess of melted metal and hardened drippings of stained solder. Their senses by now had become accustomed to the overpowering stench and the grotesque carbonized surroundings, but they weren't the least bit prepared for the hideously misshapen form on the deck.

"Oh, no!" Hunnewell gasped. He dropped his flashlight and it rolled across the deck and came to rest against the remains of a head, illuminating the skull and teeth.

"I don't envy him his death," Pitt murmured.

Hunnewell grimaced as he stooped and picked up his flashlight. Then he slipped a notebook from a pocket, held the light under his arm and flipped through several pages. "The ship sailed with six crewmen and nine passengers: fifteen in all." He fumbled a little before finding another page. "This poor devil must be the radio operator—Svendborg—Gustav Svendborg."

Pitt kneeled down and studied the body more closely. His eyes squinted and his mouth tightened. It must have been almost as he had visualized, but not quite. The scorched form was curled in the fetus position, the knees drawn up almost to the chin and the arms pulled tightly against the sides, contracted by the intense heat upon the flesh. But there was something else that caught Pitt's attention. He focused the flashlight on the deck beside the body, illuminating dimly the twisted steel legs of the radio operator's chair where they protruded from beneath his disfigured remains.

Hunnewell, his face void of all color, asked: "What do you find so interesting in that grisly thing?"

"Have a look," Pitt said. "It would seem that poor Gustav was sitting down when he died. His chair literally burned out from under him."

Hunnewell said nothing, only eyed Pitt questioningly.

"Doesn't it strike you as strange," Pitt continued, "that a man would calmly burn to death without bothering to stand up or make an effort to escape?"

"Nothing strange about it," Hunnewell said stonily. "The fire probably engulfed him while he was hunched over the transmitter sending out a Mayday." He began to choke with sickness. "We're not doing him any good with our conjectures. Let's get out of here and search the rest of the ship while I'm still able to walk."

Pitt nodded and turned and passed through the doorway. Together they made their way into the lower levels of the ship. The engine room, the galley, the salon, everywhere they went their eyes were laid on the same horrifying spectacle of death as in the radio room. By the time they discovered the thirteenth and fourteenth bodies in the wheelhouse, Hunnewell's stomach was slowly becoming immuné. He consulted his notebook several more times, marking certain pages with a pencil until only one name between the padded covers remained that didn't have a neat line drawn through it.

"That's about it," he said, snapping the book shut. "We've found them all except one. Sadly, he was the only man aboard this ship I knew."

Pitt seemed to consider for a moment. "They were all charred so far beyond recognition, he could have been any one of them."

"But he wasn't," Hunnewell said positively. "The right body won't be too difficult to identify, at least not for me." He paused. "I knew him rather well, you know."

Pitt's eyebrows raised. "No, I didn't know."

"No secret really." Hunnewell puffed on the lenses of his glasses and polished them with a handkerchief. "The man in question attended one of my classes at the Oceanographic Institute six years ago. A brilliant fellow." He motioned toward the two cremated forms on the deck. "A pity if he ended like this."

"How can you be certain you'll be able to tell him from the others?" Pitt asked.

"By his rings. He had a thing about rings. Wore them on every finger except his thumbs. Will that do?"

"It would," Pitt said thoughtfully. "But we haven't found a corpse that qualifies. We've already searched the entire ship."

"Not quite." Hunnewell pulled a slip of paper from the notebook and unfolded it under the beam of his flashlight. "This is a rough diagram of the vessel. I traced a copy from the original in the maritime archives." He pointed at the creased paper. "See here, just beyond the chartroom. A narrow ladder drops to a compartment directly beneath a false funnel. It's the only entrance."

Pitt studied the crude tracing. Then he turned and stepped outside the chartroom. "The opening is here all right. The ladder is burned, but enough of the rung bracing is left to support our weight."

The isolated compartment—situated in the exact center of the hull without portholes—was ravaged even worse than the others; the steel plating on the walls curved outward, buckled like crinkled sheets of wallpaper. It appeared empty. No trace of anything that remotely resembled furnishings was left after the conflagration. Pitt was just kneeling down, poking the ashes, searching for a sign of a body, when Hunnewell shouted.

"Here!" He fell to his knees. "Over here in the corner." Hunnewell focused the light on the sprawled outline of what had once been a man. Then he bent very low and carefully brushed away an area of the remains. When Hunnewell stood up, he held several small pieces of distorted metal in his hand.

"Not proof positive perhaps. But about as certain as we'll ever get."

Pitt took the fused bits of metal and held them under the beam of his light.

"I remember the rings quite well," Hunnewell said. "The settings were beautifully handcrafted and inlaid with eight different semiprecious stones native to Iceland. Each was carved in the likeness of an ancient Nordic god."

"Sounds impressive but a bit overdone," Pitt said.

"To you, a stranger maybe," Hunnewell returned quietly. "Yet if you had known him . . ." His voice trailed off.

Pitt eyed Hunnewell. "Do you always form sentimental attachments to your students?"

"Genius, adventurer, scientist, legend, the tenth richest man in the world before he was twenty-five. A kind and gentle person totally untouched by his fame and wealth. Yes, I think you could safely say a friendship with Kristjan Fyrie could result in a sentimental attachment."

How strange, Pitt thought. It was the first time the scientist had mentioned this man since they had left NUMA headquarters in Washington. And his name had been uttered in a hushed, almost reverent tone. The same inflection, Pitt recalled, that Admiral Sandecker had also used when he spoke of the man, reputed to be one of the most powerful figures in international finance.

Pitt looked at the twisted metal rings for a moment and then passed them back to Hunnewell.

"So this ship is the *Lax*—disappeared over a year ago with all hands, including its owner, the Icelandic mining magnate Fyrie, Kristjan Fyrie. Half the Coast Guard searched for months. Didn't find a sign. And this cremated mess is all that's left of Kristjan Fyrie. I've never seen anything like this. A ship this size couldn't vanish without a trace for nearly a year and then pop up burned to a cinder in the middle of an iceberg."

"You're quite correct, Major," Hunnewell said. "The chances are extremely remote for such an occurrence. As you know, a fire-gutted ship takes days to cool. If a current or wind pushed and held the hull against the iceberg, it would only take forty-eight hours or less before this entire ship imbedded itself under the berg's mantle. You can achieve the same situation by holding a red-hot poker against an ice block. The poker will melt its way into the block until it cools. Then the ice, if refrozen around the metal, locks it tight."

"Okay, Doc, you score on that one. However, there's one important factor no one has considered."

Pitt paused and pointed at two misshapen metal fixtures hanging from the ceiling. "A fire at sea usually starts at one location, the engine room, or a cargo hold, or a storage area, and then spreads from compartment to compartment, taking hours and sometimes days to fully consume a ship. I'll bet you any amount you care to cover that a fire investigator would scratch his head and cross this one off as a flash fire, one that totaled out the entire ship within a matter of minutes, setting a new record, ignited by causes or persons unknown."

"What do you have in mind for the cause?"

Pitt said, "A flamethrower."

There was a minute of appalled silence.

"Do you realize what you're suggesting?"

"Of course I do," Pitt said. "Right down to the violent blast of searing flame. Like it or not, a flamethrower is the logical answer."

Hunnewell stared at Pitt blankly. "I can't believe that everyone stood like sheep and let themselves be turned into human torches."

"Don't you see?" Pitt said. "Our fiendish friend somehow either drugged or poisoned the passengers and crew. Probably slipped a massive dose of chloral hydrate into their food or drinks."

"They all could have been shot," Hunnewell ventured.

"I studied several of the remains." Pitt shook his head. "There were no signs of bullets or shattered bones."

"Was it worth all this?" Hunnewell said with sickness in his eyes.

"It was to the sixteenth man." Pitt stared down at the grisly remains on the deck. "The unrecorded intruder who became the death of the party."

2

Iceland, the land of frost and fire, rugged glaciers and smoldering volcanoes, an island prism of lava-bed reds, rolling tundra greens, and placid lake blues stretched under the rich gold glow of the midnight sun. Surrounded by the Atlantic Ocean, bounded by the warm waters of the Gulf Stream in the south and by the frigid polar sea to the north, Iceland rests midway as the crow flies between New York and Moscow. To someone seeing it for the first time, Iceland seems indeed an unequaled phenomenon of beauty.

"Tell me more about Fyrie," Pitt said as he watched the jagged snow-packed peaks of the island grow on the horizon. "What was it he discovered again?"

"Zirconium." Hunnewell's gaze was lost in the distance. "Atomic number: forty."

"I barely squeaked through my geology class," Pitt said, smiling. "Why zirconium? What makes it worth killing a ship full of people over?"

"Purified zirconium is vital in the construction of

27

nuclear reactors because it absorbs little or no radia-
tion. Every nation in the world with facilities for
atomic research would give their eyeteeth to have it
obtainable by the carload. Admiral Sandecker is certain that if Fyrie and his scientists did indeed discover a vast zirconium bonanza, it was under the sea
close enough to the surface to be raised economically."

"No small undertaking," Pitt muttered, just loud
enough to be heard over the drone from the engine's
exhaust. "The problems of raising raw ore from the
sea bottom are immense."

"Yes, but not insurmountable. Fyrie Limited em-
ploys the world's leading experts at underwater mining. That's how Kristjan Fyrie built his empire, you
know, dredging diamonds off the coast of Africa. If
diamond deposits could be found on land not two
miles from shore, he reasoned, why couldn't they lie
underwater on the continental shelf? So every day
for five months he dove in the warm waters of the
Indian Ocean until he found a section of the seabed
that looked promising. The five months of diving
paid off—the dredge began to bring up high-grade
diamonds almost immediately. Within two years
Fyrie was worth forty million dollars."

Pitt noticed a dark speck in the sky, several thousand feet higher and in front of the Ulysses. "You
certainly seem to have studied the Fyrie history."

"I know it sounds strange," Hunnewell went on,
"but Fyrie seldom stayed with a project more than a
few years. Most men would have bled the operation

dry. Not Kristjan. After he made a fortune beyond his wildest dreams, he turned the whole business over to the people who financed the venture."

"Just gave it away?"

"Lock, stock and the popular barrel. He distributed every share of his stock to the native stockholders, set up a black administration that could run efficiently without him, and took the next boat back to Iceland. Of the few white men held in high esteem by the Africans, the name of Kristjan Fyrie stands right at the top."

Pitt was watching the solitary dark speck in the northern sky turn into a sleek jet aircraft. He leaned forward, screwing up his eyes against the bright blue glare. The stranger was one of the new executive jets built by the British—fast, reliable and capable of whisking twelve passengers halfway around the world in a matter of hours without a fuel stop. Pitt barely had time to realize that the stranger was painted an ebony black from nose to tail when it swept past his range of vision traveling in the opposite direction.

"Did he have a family?" Pitt asked Hunnewell.

"No, his parents died in a fire when he was very young. All he had was a twin sister. Don't really know much about her. Fyrie put her through a finishing school in Switzerland, and, so rumor has it, she later became a missionary somewhere in New Guinea. Apparently her brother's fortune meant nothing to—"

Hunnewell never finished the sentence. He jerked sideways facing Pitt, his eyes staring blankly, his mouth open in surprise but no words came out. Pitt barely had time to see the man slump forward as the plexiglass bubble encircling the cockpit shattered into a thousand jagged slivers and fell away.

Twisting to one side and throwing up an arm to protect his face from the blasting wall of cold air, Pitt momentarily lost control of the helicopter. Its aerodynamics drastically altered, the Ulysses nosed sharply upward, almost on its end, throwing Pitt and the unconscious Hunnewell violently against their backrests. It was then Pitt became aware of the machine gun shells striking the fuselage aft of the seats. The sudden uncontrolled maneuver temporarily saved their lives; the gunner aboard the black jet had been caught off guard, adjusting his trajectory too late and sending most of his fire into an empty sky.

Unable to match the helicopter's slow speed without stalling, the mysterious jet soared forward and swung around in a hundred-and-eighty-degree turn for another assault. Pitt struggled to bring the helicopter on a level course, a near impossible task with a two-hundred-mile-an-hour air stream tearing at his eyes. He throttled down, trying desperately to reduce the unseen force that pinned his body against the seat.

Pitt didn't kid himself. There was no escape; the battle was too one-sided. A grim smile wrinkled around Pitt's eyes as he lowered the copter to a bare twenty feet above the water. Victory was hopeless, but there was a slight chance of a tie score. Pitt steadied the small defenseless craft and hovered as the jet dove like a concrete bird, directly toward him.

Pitt braced himself for the impact and threw the

Ulyssess straight up into the attacking plane, the helicopter's rotor blades shattering as they sliced through the jet's horizontal stabilizer. Instinctively Pitt flicked the ignition switch off as the turbine engine, without the drag from the rotor, raced wildly amid the howl of tortured metal. Then the racket stopped, and the sky was silent except for the wind that whistled in Pitt's ears.

He snatched a glance at the strange jet just before it crashed into the sea, nose first, its tail section hanging like a broken arm. Pitt and the unconscious Hunnewell weren't much better off. All they could do was sit and wait for the crippled helicopter to drop like a stone nearly seventy feet into the cold Atlantic water.

When the crash came, it was much worse than Pitt had anticipated. The Ulysses fell on its side into the Iceland surf in six feet of water, a scant football field length from shore. Pitt's head whipped sideways and glanced off the door frame, sending him into a vortex of darkness. Fortunately the agonizing shock of the icy water jolted him back to dizzy wakefulness. Waves of nausea swept over him, and he knew he was only a hairbreadth away from drifting off to sleep for the last time.

His face twisted with pain, Pitt undid his seat belt and shoulder harness, taking a gulp of air before a breaking wave crest passed over the helicopter, then quickly he unfastened Hunnewell and lifted his head above the swirling water. At that instant, Pitt slipped and lost his balance as a crashing breaker knocked him from the Ulysses into the surf. Still grasping

Hunnewell by a death grip on the coat collar, he battled the rolling surge as it swept him toward shore, rolling him end-over-end across the uneven rocky bottom.

If Pitt ever wondered what it was like to drown, he had a pretty good idea now. The freezing water stung every square inch of his skin like a million bees. His ears failed to pop, and his head was one tormenting ache; his nostrils filled with water, and the thin membranes of his lungs felt as if they'd been dipped in nitric acid. Finally, after bashing his knees into a bed of rocks, he struggled to his feet, his head bursting gratefully into the pure Icelandic air. He staggered from the water onto a pebble-strewn beach, half carrying, half dragging Hunnewell.

A few steps beyond the tideline Pitt eased his burden down and checked the doctor's pulse and breathing; both were on the fast side but regular. Then he saw Hunnewell's left arm. It had been terribly mangled at the elbow by the machine gun bullets. As quickly as his numbed hands would allow, Pitt took off his shirt, tore off the sleeves, and tightly wrapped them around the wound to stem the flow of blood. Then he sat Hunnewell up against a large rock, made a crude sling, and elevated the wound to aid the control of bleeding.

Pitt could do nothing more for his friend, so he lay down on the lumpy carpet of stone and let the unwelcome pain in his body and the hated currents of nausea sweep through his body. Relaxing as much as the sickness would let him, he closed his eyes, shutting out a magnificent view of the cloud-dotted Arctic sky. Just then, Hunnewell moaned softly. Pitt leaned over him, cradling the bald head. The old man was conscious now. He was breathing heavily and tried to speak, but the words caught in his throat. There was a strange kind of serenity in his eyes as he gripped Pitt's hand, and in a strained effort murmured, "God save thee—" Then he trembled and gave a little gasp.

Dr. Hunnewell was dead.

3

Time after time, Pitt struggled up from the bottom of the rolling surf and staggered onto the beach dragging Hunnewell. Time after time, he bandaged the oceanographer's arm only to slide into darkness again. Desperately, every time the event ran through his brain like an image from a film projector, he tried to hang onto those fleeting moments of consciousness, only to lose out to the inevitable fact that nothing can change the past. It was a nightmare, he thought vaguely as he tried to tear himself away from the bloodstained beach. He gathered his strength and with a mighty effort forced his eyes open, expecting to see an empty bedroom.

"Good morning, Dirk," said a soft voice. "I'd almost lost hope that you would ever wake up."

Pitt looked up into the smiling brown eyes of Tidi Royal, Admiral Sandecker's private secretary.

Pitt pulled himself to a sitting position. "If you're here, it could only mean the admiral is close by."

"Fifteen minutes after you crashed, we were on a

34

jet to Iceland. He's pretty shaken about Dr. Hunnewell's death. Admiral Sandecker blames himself."

"He's going to have to stand in line," Pitt said. "I got there first." He frowned quizzically. "What time is it?" he asked.

"A few minutes past ten—A.M. I might add."

"I've wasted nearly fourteen hours. What happened to my clothes?"

"Thrown out in the trash, I imagine. They weren't fit for rags."

"In that case, how about rounding up something casual while I take a quick shower."

Exactly two hours later, clad in well-fitting slacks and sport shirt, Pitt sat across a desk from Admiral James Sandecker. The admiral looked tired and old, far beyond his years. His red hair was tousled in a shaggy unkempt mane, and it was obvious from the stubble on his chin and cheeks that he hadn't shaved for at least two days. He held one of his massive cigars casually in the fingers of his right hand. He grunted something about being glad to see Pitt alive and still connected in all the right places. The weary, bloodshot eyes studied Pitt intently.

"Your story, Dirk. Let's have it."

Pitt slouched back in his chair. "Well, it's more your story than mine. A dim, nearly undistinguishable outline of a ship turns up in an iceberg. The Coast Guard doesn't have the slightest idea what registry it is. Yet four days go by and there is no investigation. Why? Somebody in the capitol with the authority, high authority, ordered hands off, that's why."

Sandecker toyed with the cigar. "I suppose you know what you're talking about, Major?"

"Well, no . . . sir," Pitt answered. "Without the facts, I'm guessing. But you and Hunnewell didn't guess. There wasn't the slightest doubt in your minds that the derelict was the *Lax,* a ship that had been listed as missing for over a year. You had absolute proof. How or where it came from I can't say, but you had it."

Pitt's green eyes blazed into Sandecker's. "At this point my crystal ball gets foggy. I was surprised, but Hunnewell was genuinely stunned when we found that the *Lax* was burned to junk. This factor wasn't in the script, was it, Admiral? In fact, everything, including your well-planned scheme, began to go down the drain. Someone you didn't count on was working against you. Someone with resources you or whatever agency in our government that is co-operating with you never considered.

"You lost control. You're up against a shrewd mind, Admiral. And the message is written in neon lights, this guy doesn't play for ice cream and cake at birthday parties. He kills people like an exterminator kills termites. The name of the game is zirconium. I don't buy it. People might kill one or two persons for a fortune, but not in wholesale lots. Hunnewell was your friend for many years, Admiral, mine for only a few days, and I lost him. He was my responsibility and I failed. His contributions to soci-

ety outstrip anything I'm capable of. Better I'd have
died on that beach instead of him."

Sandecker showed no reaction to any of this. His
unblinking eyes never left Pitt's face as he sat behind
the desk thoughtfully tapping the fingers of his right
hand on the glass top. Then he stood up, came
around the desk and put his hands on Pitt's shoulders. "It was a miracle you both made it to shore.
I'm the one to blame. I had a hint of what was going
to happen and I wasn't smart enough to read the
cards. I didn't deal you in on the action because it
wasn't necessary. You were the best man I could lay
my hands on for a tricky chauffeur job. As soon as
you got Hunnewell here to Reykjavik, I was going to
put you on the next flight back to California." He
paused to check his watch. "There's an Air Force reconnaissance jet leaving for Tyler Field, New Jersey,
in one hour and six minutes. You can make connections for the West Coast when you get there."

"No, thanks, Admiral." Pitt rose from the chair
and walked to the window, staring over the city's
peaked and sun-splashed roofs. "I've heard that Iceland is quite beautiful. I'd like to see for myself."

"I can make that an order."

"No good, sir. I understand what you're trying to
do, and I'm grateful. The attempt on my life and
Hunnewell's was only half successful. I'd like to stick
around and see if our attackers try to finish the job."

"Sorry, Dirk." Sandecker was back on friendly
terms again. "I'm not going to throw your life away
with the wave of a hand. Before I stand at your

graveside, I'll have you locked up and standing in front of a court-martial for willful destruction of government property."

Sandecker sat at his desk again. "Okay, you've told me my story, now I want to hear yours—from the beginning." He peered at Pitt with an expression that dared argument. "Shall we commence?"

Sandecker heard Pitt out, then said: " 'God save thee,' that's what he said?"

"That's all he said. Then he was gone. I'd hoped Dr. Hunnewell might have offered me a clue to the whereabouts of the *Lax* between the time it vanished and the time it became inbedded in the iceberg, but he volunteered nothing except a historical sketch of Kristjan Fyrie and a lecture on zirconium."

"He did as he was told. I didn't want you involved."

"That was two days ago. Now I'm involved up to my neck." Pitt leaned over the desk toward the older man. "Let's have it, you sly old fox. What is going on?"

Sandecker grinned. "For your sake, I'm going to take that as a compliment." He pulled out a bottom drawer and propped his feet on it. "I hope you know what you're letting yourself in for."

"I don't have the vaguest idea, but tell me anyway."

"All right then." Sandecker leaned back in his swivel chair and puffed several times on his cigar. "About a year and a half ago, Fyrie's scientists successfully designed and constructed a nuclear undersea probe that could identify fifteen to twenty different mineral elements on the ocean floor. The probe operated by briefly exposing the metallic elements to neutrons given off by a laboratory-produced element called celtinium-279. When activated by the neutrons, the elements on the ocean's bottom gave off gamma rays, which were then analyzed and counted by a tiny detector on the probe. During tests off Iceland, the probe detected and measured mineral samples of manganese, gold, nickel, titanium, and zirconium—the zirconium in huge and unheard-of amounts."

"I think I see. Without the probe, the zirconium could never be found again," Pitt said thoughtfully. "The prize then is not the rare elements, but rather the probe itself."

"Yes, the probe opens a vast and untapped frontier for undersea mining. Whoever owns it won't control the world, of course, but possession could lead to a direct reshuffling of private financial empires and a healthy shot in the arm for the treasury of any country with a continental shelf containing a rich storehouse of minerals."

Pitt was silent for a few moments. "But is it worth all the killing?"

Sandecker hesitated. "It depends upon how bad somebody wants it. There are men who wouldn't kill for every cent in the world, and there are others who wouldn't hesitate to slit a throat for the price of a meal."

"In Washington, you informed me that Fyrie and his scientific team were on their way to the U.S. to open negotiations with our defense contractors. I take it that was a little white lie?"

Sandecker smiled. "Yes, that was actually an understatement. Fyrie was scheduled to meet with the President and present him with the probe. I was the first one Fyrie notified when the tests on the probe proved successful. I don't know what Hunnewell told you about Fyrie, but he was a visionary, a gentle man who wouldn't step on an ant or a flower. He knew the far-reaching good the probe would bring to mankind; he also knew what unscrupulous interests would do to exploit it once the probe fell into their hands, so he decided to turn it over to the nation that he was certain would make beneficial and charitable use of its potential."

Pitt grinned knowingly. It was a well-advertised fact that Admiral Sandecker, in spite of his tough exterior, was at heart a humanitarian, and he rarely disguised his disgust and hatred for greed-driven industrialists.

"Isn't it possible," Pitt asked, "for American engineers to develop our own probe?"

"Yes, in fact we already have one, but compared with Fyrie's probe, it operates with all the efficiency of a bicycle next to a sportscar. His people made a breakthrough that is ten years ahead of anything we or the Russians are currently developing."

"Any ideas on who stole the probe?"

Sandecker shook his head. "None. It's obviously a well-financed organization. Beyond that we're playing blindman's bluff in a swamp."

"A foreign country would have the necessary resources to—"

"You can forget that," Sandecker interrupted. "The National Intelligence Agency is positive no foreign government is in the act. Any country would think twice before killing two dozen people over an innocent, nondestructive scientific instrument. No, it's got to be a private motive. For what purpose besides financial gain," he shrugged helplessly, "we can't even guess."

"All right, so the mysterious organization has the probe, so they strike a bonanza on the sea floor. How do they raise it?"

"They can't," Sandecker replied. "Not without highly technical equipment."

"It doesn't make sense. If they've had the probe over a year, what good has it done them?"

"They've put the probe to good use all right," Sandecker said seriously, "testing every square foot of the continental shelf on the Atlantic shore of North and South America. And they used the *Lax* to do it."

Pitt stared at him curiously. "The *Lax?* I don't follow."

"Do you remember Dr. Len Matajic and his assistant, Jack O'Riley?"

Pitt frowned, recalling. "I air-dropped supplies to them three months ago when they set up camp on an ice floe in Baffin Bay. Dr. Matajic was studying currents below a depth of ten thousand feet, trying to prove a pet theory of his that a deep layer of warm water had the capacity to melt the Pole if only one percent of it could be diverted upward."

"What was the last you heard of them?"

Pitt shrugged. "I left for the Oceanlab Project in California as soon as they began routine housekeeping. Why ask me? You planned and coordinated their expedition."

"Yes, I planned the expedition," Sandecker repeated slowly. "Matajic and O'Riley are dead. The plane bringing them back from the ice floe crashed in the sea. No trace was found."

"Strange, I hadn't heard. It must have just happened."

Sandecker put another match to his cigar. "A month ago yesterday, to be exact."

Pitt stared at him. "Why the secrecy? Nothing was in print or in broadcast about their accident. As your special projects director, I should have been one of the first to be informed."

"Only one other man besides myself was aware of their deaths—the radio operator who took their last message. I've made no announcement because I intend to bring them back from their watery grave."

"Sorry, Admiral," Pitt said. "You've lost me completely."

"All right then," Sandecker said heavily. "Five weeks ago I received a signal from Matajic. Seems O'Riley, while on a scouting trek, spotted a fishing trawler that had moored to the north end of their ice floe. Not being socially aggressive, he returned to base and informed Matajic. Then together, they trudged back and paid a friendly call on the fishermen to determine if they needed assistance. An odd bunch, Matajic said. The ship flew the flag of Iceland, yet most of the crew were Arabs, while the rest represented at least six different countries including the United States. It seems a bearing had burned out in their diesel engine. Rather than drift around while repairs were made, they decided to tie up on the ice floe to let the crew stretch their legs."

"Nothing suspicious in that," Pitt commented.

"The captain and crew invited Matajic and O'Riley on board for dinner," Sandecker continued. "This courteous act seemed harmless enough at the time. Later, it was seen as an obvious attempt to avoid suspicion. By sheer coincidence, it backfired."

"So our two scientists were also on the list to see something they shouldn't have."

"You guessed it. Some years previously, Kristjan Fyrie had entertained Dr. Hunnewell and Dr. Matajic aboard his yacht. The exterior of the trawler had been altered, of course, but the instant Matajic stepped into the main salon, he recognized the ship as the *Lax*. If he had said nothing, he and O'Riley might have been alive today. Unfortunately, he innocently asked why the proud and plush *Lax* that he remembered had been converted into a common fishing trawler. It was an honest question, but one that had cruel consequences."

Sandecker reached inside his breast pocket and pulled out a worn and folded piece of paper. "This is Matajic's last message."

Pitt took the paper from the admiral's hand and unfolded it across the desk. It read: MAYDAY! MAYDAY! ATTACKED. BLACK. NUMBER ONE ENGINE IS . . . The words abruptly ended.

"Enter the black jet."

"Exactly. With his only witnesses out of the way, the captain's problem was now the Coast Guard, whom he was sure would show up at any moment."

Pitt looked at Sandecker speculatively. "But the Coast Guard didn't come. They were never invited. You've yet to explain why you maintained silence even after you were certain three of NUMA's men were killed."

"At the time I didn't really know." The vagueness wasn't like Sandecker. Normally he was as decisive and direct as a bolt of lightning. "I suppose I didn't want them to have the satisfaction of knowing how successful they were—I thought it best to let them wonder."

"How did you handle the search party?"

"I notified all search and rescue units in the Northern Command that a valuable piece of equipment had fallen off of a NUMA research ship and was floating around lost. I gave out the course the plane would have taken and waited for a sighting report. There was none." Sandecker waved his cigar to indicate helplessness. "I also waited in vain for the sighting of a trawler matching the hull design of the *Lax*. It too had evaporated."

"That's why you were dead sure it was the *Lax* under the iceberg."

"Let's just say I was eighty percent certain," Sandecker said. "I also did a bit of checking with every port authority between Buenos Aires and Goose Bay, Labrador. Twelve ports recorded the entry and departure of an Icelandic fishing trawler matching the *Lax*'s altered superstructure. For what it's worth, it went under the name of *Surtsey*. *Surtsey*, by the way, is Icelandic for 'submarine.' "

"I see." Pitt said.

Sandecker paused. "If you're wondering why NUMA is mixed up in this instead of sitting on the sidelines and cheering on the National Intelligence Agency and their army of super spies, the answer is, or I should say was, Hunnewell. He corresponded with Fyrie's scientists for months, offering his knowledge toward the ultimate success of the probe. It was Hunnewell who was instrumental in the development of celtinium-279. Only he had a rough idea of what the probe looked like, and only he could have safely disassembled it."

"That, of course, explains why Hunnewell had to be the first aboard the derelict."

"Yes, celtinium in its refined state is very unstable. Under the right conditions, it can explode with a force equal to a fifty-ton phosphate bomb, but with a pronounced characteristic difference. Celtinium fulminates at a very slow rate, burning everything in its path to ashes. Yet, unlike more common explosives, its expansion pressure is quite low, about the same as a sixty-mile-an-hour wind. It could go off and melt but not shatter a pane of glass."

"Then my flamethrower theory was a bust. It was the probe that went off and turned the *Lax* into an instant pyre."

Sandecker smiled. "You came close."

"But that means the probe is destroyed."

Sandecker nodded, his smile rapidly fading. "All of it, the murders, the probe, the killers' search for undersea treasure, it went all for nothing—a terrible, terrible waste."

He paused, then went on almost absently. "A lot of good it will do them. Hunnewell was the only person on earth with the process for celtinium-279. As he often said, it was basically so simple that he kept it in his head."

"The fools," Pitt murmured. "They murdered their only key to constructing a new probe. But why? Hunnewell couldn't have been a serious threat unless he found something on the derelict that led to the organization and its mastermind."

"I haven't the vaguest idea." Sandecker shrugged helplessly. "Anymore than I can guess who the unseen men were who chipped the red dye marker off the iceberg."

"I wish I knew where to take the next step," Pitt said.

"I've taken care of that little matter for you. There's someone I want you to meet."

"Oh, really?" Pitt suddenly came alive. "Who?"

"Kirsti," Sandecker said with a sly smile. "Kirsti Fyrie, Kristjan Fyrie's twin sister."

4

Pitt surveyed the crowded dining hall filled with laughing, talkative Icelanders. He was standing there, his eyes taking in the scene, his nostrils basking in the rich food smells when the maitre d' came up and spoke in Icelandic. Pitt shook his head and pointed at Admiral Sandecker and Tidi Royal comfortably ensconced at a table. He made his way over to them.

Sandecker waved Pitt to a chair opposite Tidi. "You're ten minutes late."

"Sorry," Pitt said. "I took a walk in the Tjarnargardar gardens and did a little sightseeing. Where is this exciting person I've heard so much about?" Pitt asked as he sat down.

"Miss Fyrie should be along any minute," Sandecker replied.

"Just before we were attacked, Hunnewell said that Fyrie's sister was a missionary in New Guinea."

"Yes, little else is known about her. In fact, few people knew she even existed until Fyrie's will named her sole beneficiary. Then she appeared at

Fyrie Limited one day and took the reins as smoothly as if she had built the empire herself. She's shrewd—just as shrewd as her brother was."

Sandecker watched as the waiter set water down in front of them and was several tables away before he turned back to Pitt. "Nearly forty percent of NUMA's projects are designed and planned around mining the sea floor. Russia leads us by a wide margin in surface programs, the science of her fishing fleet far surpasses anything we've got. But she lags badly in deep submersibles—a vital piece of equipment for undersea mining. This is our strong point. We want to maintain this advantage. Our country has the resources, but Fyrie Limited has the technical knowledge. With Kristjan Fyrie we had a good, close working association. Now that he's only a memory, I don't care to see the results of our efforts lost just when our programs are on the verge of hitting paydirt. I've talked to Miss Fyrie. All of a sudden she's very noncommittal—says she has decided to reevaluate her firm's programs with our country."

"You said she's shrewd," Pitt said. "Maybe she's holding out to the highest bidder. There's nothing in the book that says she has to be as magnanimous as her brother."

"Anything is possible. Maybe she hates Americans." Sandecker said irritably. "There must be a reason, and we've got to find it."

"Enter Dirk Pitt, stage left."

"Precisely. I'm taking you off the Pacific Oceanlab project indefinitely and putting you on this one. Forget playing secret agent while you're at it. Leave the intrigue and the dead bodies to the National Intelligence Agency. You're to act in your official capacity as special projects director for NUMA. No more, no less. If you stumble onto any information that might lead to the people who killed Fyrie, Hunnewell, and Matajic, you're to pass it on."

Sandecker took a long swallow from his glass. "I've arranged an exchange program. I'm taking one of their top engineers with me to the States to observe and study our techniques while you're to stay here and report on theirs. Your primary job will be to restore the close relationship we once enjoyed with the Fyrie's management."

"If this Fyrie woman has been so cool toward you and NUMA, why did she consent to meet us tonight?"

"Dr. Hunnewell and her brother were good friends. His death and the fact that you made a gallant but losing attempt to save his life played on her emotions. In short, she insisted on meeting you."

"I can't wait to meet my new boss face to face," Pitt said.

Sandecker nodded. "You can in precisely five seconds—she just walked in."

Pitt turned, and so did every other male head in the restaurant. She stood in the foyer very tall and very blond, incredibly beautiful. Now she caught Sandecker's wave, and she walked over to the table, moving with a graceful flowing motion that possessed all the suppleness of a ballerina and more than the suggestion of a natural athlete.

Pitt pushed back his chair and rose and studied her face as she approached. It was her tan that intrigued him. The delicately clear tanned complexion somehow seemed foreign to an Icelandic woman, even one who spent a good portion of her life in the back country of New Guinea. The total effect was striking.

"My dear Miss Fyrie, I'm honored that you could dine with us." Admiral Sandecker took her hand and kissed it. Then he turned to Tidi. "May I introduce my secretary, Miss Tidi Royal."

The two women exchanged polite greetings.

Then Sandecker turned to Pitt. "And this is Major Dirk Pitt, the real driving force behind my agency's projects."

"So this is the brave gentleman you've told me so much about, Admiral. I am deeply sorry for the tragic loss of Dr. Hunnewell. My brother thought very highly of him."

"We're sorry too," Pitt said.

There was a pause while they looked at each other, Kirsti Fyrie with a touch of speculation in her eyes, Pitt with analytical appraisal.

"Please allow me to introduce you to our native buffet dishes," Kirsti said.

"I thought you'd never offer!" Pitt laughed. He rose and pulled back Kirsti's chair.

The varieties of fish seemed endless. Pitt counted over twenty different dishes of salmon and nearly fifteen of cod alone. They each returned with their plates heaped with near over-the-rim helpings.

The meal was eaten with an exchange of small talk, everyone relaxed and comfortable in the atmosphere of friendliness and good food. Two hours later, during a strawberry and ice cream flambé, especially concocted by Pitt and an agreeable chef, Kirsti began to make apologies for an early departure.

"I hope you will not think me rude, Admiral Sandecker, but I am afraid I must leave you, Miss Royal, and Major Pitt very shortly. My fiancé has insisted on taking me to a poetry reading tonight."

Admiral Sandecker beamed a smile. "My sincerest wishes for your happiness, Miss Fyrie. I had no idea you were engaged. Who is the lucky man?"

"Rondheim—Oskar Rondheim," Kristi announced. "My brother introduced us in a letter. Oskar and I exchanged pictures and corresponded for two years before we finally met."

Sandecker stared at her. "Wait a minute," he said slowly. "I think I know of him. Isn't he the one who owns an international chain of canneries? Rondheim Industries? A fishing fleet the size of Spain's navy? Or am I thinking of some other Rondheim?"

"No, that's right," Kirsti said. "His executive offices are right here in Reykjavik."

"The fishing boats, painted blue, flying a red flag with an albatross?" Pitt inquired.

Kirsti nodded. "The albatross is Oskar's good luck symbol. Do you know his boats?"

"I've had occasion to fly over them," Pitt said.

Of course Pitt knew the boats and their symbol. So did every fisherman of every country north of the fortieth parallel. Rondheim's fishing fleets were notorious for wiping out fishing grounds, almost to the verge of extinction, robbing the nets of the other fishermen, and dropping their own distinctive red-dyed nets inside the territorial boundaries of other countries.

"A merger between Fyrie Limited and Rondheim Industries would result in a most powerful empire," Sandecker said slowly, almost as if he were weighing the consequences.

Pitt's mind was running along the same channels. Suddenly, his train of thought was broken when Kirsti waved her hand.

"There he is. There!"

They turned and followed Kirsti's gaze to a tall, snow-haired, distinguished-looking figure vigorously stepping toward them. Rondheim stopped before the table, his even white teeth flashing in a seemingly cordial smile. "Kirsti darling. How delightful you look tonight." Then he affectionately embraced her.

Kirsti introduced Sandecker.

"It is indeed a pleasure to meet you, Admiral," Rondheim said, a cool look in his eyes. "Your reputation as a mariner and oceanographer is widely known throughout seafaring circles."

"Your reputation is also widely known throughout seafaring circles, Mr. Rondheim." The admiral shook Rondheim's hand and turned to Pitt. "Major Dirk Pitt, my special projects director."

Rondheim paused a moment, making a professional assessment of the man standing before him before he extended his hand, "Major Pitt."

"How do you do." Pitt gritted his teeth as Rondheim's hand closed like a vise. Pitt fought a desire to squeeze back; instead he let his hand go limp in a dead fish grip. "Good heavens, Mr. Rondheim, you're a very strong man."

"I'm sorry, Major." Rondheim jerked his hand back as though he had been shocked by an electrical circuit. "The men who work for me are a rugged breed and have to be treated as such. When I am off the deck of a fishing boat, I sometimes forget to act like a gentleman of the land."

"Mr. Rondheim, you needn't apologize. No harm done as long as I can still wield a brush."

"Do you paint, Major?" Kirsti asked.

"Yes, landscapes mostly."

Kirsti looked at Pitt curiously. "I would love to see your work sometime."

"Unfortunately all of my canvases are in Washington. However, I'd be delighted to present you with my impressions of Iceland while I'm here."

"You are very kind, but I could not accept—"

"Nonsense," Pitt interrupted. "Your coastline is magnificent. I'm simply dying to see if I can capture its contrasting forces of sea and rock meeting one another in a natural eruption of light and color."

Kirsti smiled politely. "If you insist, but you must permit me to do something for you in return."

"I ask one favor—a boat. To do your shoreline

justice, I must sketch it from the sea. Nothing fancy. Any small cruiser will do."

"See my dockmaster, Major. He will have a cruiser ready for you." She hesitated a moment as Rondheim loomed up and placed his hand on her shoulder. "Our boats are moored at Pier Twelve."

"Come, darling," Rondheim said. "Max is reading his new anthology tonight. We must not be late." His hand tightened, and she closed her eyes. "I hope you good people will excuse us."

"Yes, of course," Sandecker said. "It's been a very enjoyable two hours, Miss Fyrie. Thank you for joining us."

Before anyone could say anything further, Rondheim hooked his hand through Kirsti's arm and led her from the dining room.

As soon as they passed beyond the door, Pitt leaned forward, elbows on the table, his face dead serious. "He's your reason behind Fyrie's sudden reluctance to cooperate with the United States and NUMA. The man is no dummy. Once he marries Kirsti Fyrie, control of two of the largest privately owned corporations in the world will come under one roof. The possibilities are immense. Iceland and its government are too small, too dependent on the future Fyrie-Rondheim cartel for its economy to offer even a token resistance against a highly financed takeover. Then, with the right strategy, the Faeroe Islands and Greenland, giving Rondheim virtual control over the North Atlantic. After that, one can only guess in which direction his ambitions lie."

Sandecker shook his head. "You're assuming too much. Kirsti Fyrie would never go along with an international power play."

"She will have no choice in the matter," Pitt said.

Tidi nodded. "I agree with Dirk. She was terrified of him."

Sandecker looked at her speculatively. "What do you mean by that?"

"Just what I said," Tidi said firmly. "Miss Fyrie was scared to death of Mr. Rondheim. Didn't you see how tightly he squeezed her shoulder?"

"Are you sure you're not imagining or exaggerating?"

Tidi shook her head. "It was all she could do to keep from screaming."

Sandecker's eyes were suddenly full of hostility. He gazed at Pitt steadily. "Did you catch it?"

"Yes."

"I'd like to think you have a hazy idea of what you're doing with that *artiste* act," Sandecker said grimly. "I know for a fact that you can't draw a straight line. Natural eruption of light—my eye."

"I don't have to. Tidi will handle that little chore for me. I've seen samples of her work. It's quite good."

"I do abstracts," Tidi said, a pained look on her face. "I've never tried a true-life seascape."

"Fake it," Pitt said briskly. "Do an abstract seascape. We're not out to impress the head curator at the Louvre."

"But I have no supplies," Tidi protested. "Besides,

the admiral and I are leaving for Washington the day after tomorrow."

"Your flight has just been canceled." Pitt turned to Sandecker. "Right, Admiral?"

Sandecker folded his hands and mulled for a few moments. "In view of what we've learned in the last five minutes, I think it best if I hang around for a few days."

"The change of climate will do you good," Pitt said. "You might even get in a fishing trip."

Sandecker studied Pitt's face. "Painting classes, fishing expeditions. Would you humor an old man and tell me what's running through that agile mind of yours?"

Pitt picked up a glass of water and swilled the lucid contents. "A black airplane," he said quietly. "A black airplane resting beneath a watery death shroud."

5

They found Pier Twelve at about ten in the morning and were passed through the entrance barrier by a Fyrie guard. Tidi held a sketching pad under one arm and a satchel-sized handbag under the other.

"Hi," Pitt said to the guard. "Miss Fyrie has generously loaned us the use of one of her boats. Which one is it?"

Without a word the guard led them down the pier, stopping in a hundred feet and pointing down at a gleaming thirty-two-foot Chris Craft cruiser.

Pitt leaped aboard and disappeared below. In a minute he was back on the pier. "No, no, this won't do at all. Too mundane, too ostentatious. To create properly I must have a creative atmosphere." He looked across the pier. "There, how about that one?"

Before the guard could reply, Pitt trotted the width of the pier and dropped to the deck of a decrepit-looking forty-foot fishing boat. He explored it briefly, then popped his head through a hatchway.

"This is perfect. It has character, a crude uniqueness. We'll take this one."

The guard hesitated for a moment. Finally, with a shrug, he nodded and left them, walking along the pier back to the entrance, throwing a backward look at Pitt every so often and shaking his head.

When he was out of earshot, Tidi said, "Why this old dirty tub? Why not that nice yacht?"

"Dirk knows what he's doing." Sandecker set the rod and tackle box down on the worn deck planking and looked at Pitt. "Does it have a fathometer?"

"A Fleming six-ten, the top of the line. Extrasensitive frequencies for detecting fish at different depths." Pitt motioned down a narrow companionway. "This boat was a lucky choice. Let me show you the engine room, Admiral."

"You mean we ignored that beautiful Chris Craft simply because it doesn't have a fathometer?" Tidi asked disappointedly.

"That's right," Pitt answered. "A fathometer is our only hope of finding the black plane."

Pitt turned and led Sandecker through the companionway down into the engine room. The stale air and the dank smell of oil and bilge immediately filled their nostrils, making them gasp at the drastic change from the diamond-pure atmosphere above. There was another odor. Sandecker looked at Pitt questioningly.

"Gas fumes?"

Pitt nodded. "Take a look at the engines."

A diesel engine is the most efficient means of propelling a small boat, particularly a fishing boat.

Heavy, low revolutions-per-minute, slow but cheap to run and reliable, the diesel is used in nearly every workboat on the sea that doesn't rely on sails for power—that is, except this boat. Sitting side by side, their propeller shafts vanishing into the bilge, a pair of Sterling 420 h.p. gas-fed engines gleamed in the dim light of the engine room like sleeping giants awaiting the starting switch to goad them into thunderous action.

"What would a scow like this be doing with all this power?" Sandecker queried quietly.

"Unless I miss my guess," Pitt murmured, "the guard goofed."

"Meaning?"

"On a shelf in the main cabin I found a pennant with an albatross on it."

Pitt ran a hand over one of the Sterling's intake manifolds; it was clean enough to pass a naval inspection. "This boat belongs to Rondheim, not Fyrie."

Sandecker thought for a moment. "Miss Fyrie instructed us to see her dockmaster. For some unknown reason he was absent. It makes one wonder if we weren't set up."

"I don't think so," Pitt said. "Rondheim will undoubtedly keep a tight eye on us, but we've given him no cause to be suspicious of our actions—not yet, at any rate. The guard made an honest mistake. Without special instructions he probably figured we were given permission to select any boat on the pier, so he quite naturally showed us the best of the lot first. There was nothing in the script that said we would pick this little gem."

"What is it doing here? Rondheim surely can't be hard up for dock space."

"Who cares," Pitt said, a wide grin stretching his features. "As long as the keys are in the ignition, I suggest we take it and run before the guard changes his mind."

The admiral needed no persuasion. "Cast off the lines, Major. I'm anxious to see what these Sterlings can do."

Precisely one minute later, the guard came running down the pier waving his arms like crazy. It was too late. Pitt stood on the deck and waved back good-naturedly as Sandecker, happy as a child with a new toy, gunned the engines and steered the deceptive-looking boat out into Reykjavik harbor.

Sandecker eased the throttles back a notch above idle and took *The Grimsi* on a slow, leisurely tour of Reykjavik harbor. Before leaving the harbor they tied up at a bait boat and purchased two buckets of herring. Then, after an animated conversation with the bait fishermen, they cast off and headed toward the sea.

As soon as they rounded a rocky point and lost sight of the harbor, Sandecker eased open the throttles and slowly pushed *The Grimsi* to thirty knots. The waves began to melt together as *The Grimsi* increased speed and lost them behind her swirling wake. Pitt found a chart of the coast and laid it on a small shelf beside Sandecker.

"It's right about here." Pitt tapped a spot on the map with a pencil. "Twenty miles southeast of Keflavik."

"Are you sure of your search pattern?" Sandecker asked.

"Twenty percent certain, eighty percent guesswork," Pitt answered. "I could have lowered the odds if I had the Ulysses as a checkpoint."

Sandecker paused to make a course change. "Have you checked the diving gear?"

"Yes, it's all accounted for. Remind me to thank those State Department people at the consulate when we get back. Dressing up and playing bait fishermen took a bit of doing on such short notice. To anyone gawking through a pair of navy binoculars it could have only looked an innocent encounter. The diving gear was slipped on board so smoothly and inconspicuously while you were going through the routine of bait buying that I almost missed detecting the transfer from ten feet away."

"I don't like the action. Diving alone invites danger, and danger invites death. I'll have you know I'm not in the habit of going against my own orders and allowing one of my men to dive in unknown waters without the proper precautions." Sandecker shifted from one foot to the other. He was going against his better judgment, and the discomfort showed clearly in his expression. "What do you hope to find down there besides a broken black airplane and bloated bodies?"

"That plane, Admiral, is the only positive lead we have to Hunnewell's and Matajic's murderer. The one thing black paint can't cover is the serial number of an engine, at least not on the turbine casing under the cowling. If we find the plane, and if I can retrieve the digits, it then becomes a simple matter to contact the manufacturer, trace the engine to the plane, and from there to the owner—"

Pitt broke off suddenly, his eyes concentrating on the graph and stylus of the fathometer he was using to calculate the ocean depth. The black lines began widening from a thin waver back and forth across the paper to a small mountainlike sweep that indicated a sudden rise of eight to ten feet above the flat, sandy sea floor.

"I think we've got it," Pitt said calmly. "Circle to port and cross our wake on course one-eight-five, Admiral."

Sandecker spun the helm and made a two-hundred-and-seventy-degree swing to the south, causing *The Grimsi* to rock gently as it passed over the waves of its own wake. This time the stylus took longer to sweep to a height of ten feet before tapering back to zero.

"What depth?" Sandecker asked.

"One hundred and forty-five feet," Pitt replied. "Judging from the indication, we just passed over her from wing tip to wing tip."

Minutes later, *The Grimsi* was moored over the reading on the fathometer. The shore was nearly a mile away, the great cliffs showing off their gray vertical rock more distinctly than ever under the northern sun. At the same time, a slight breeze sprang up and began to ruffle the surface of the rolling water. It was a mild warning, a signal foretelling the beginning of rougher weather to come. With the breeze a state of chilling apprehension raised the hairs on Pitt's neck. For the first time he began to wonder what he would find beneath the cold Atlantic waters.

6

The brilliant blue sky, free of clouds, allowed the sun to beat down and turn Pitt's black neoprene wet suit into a skintight sauna bath as he checked the old single-hose U.S. Diver's Deepstar regulator. He considered himself lucky that one of the young consulate members made a sport of diving and had the equipment on hand. He attached the regulator to the valve of an air bottle. Two single tanks were all he could scrounge. Enough for fifteen minutes' diving, and even that was stretching precious time for dives to one hundred and forty feet. His only consolation was that he wouldn't be down long enough to worry about decompression.

His last look of *The Grimsi*'s deck before the blue-green water closed over his face mask was of Admiral Sandecker sitting sleepily with fishing pole gripped in both hands and Tidi studiously sketching the Icelandic shoreline. Shielded from anyone watching from the cliffs, Pitt slipped over the side behind the wheelhouse and became a part of the sea's vastness. His body was tense. Without a diving companion there was no margin for error.

The shock of the icy water against his sweating body nearly made him pass out. Using the anchor line as a guide, he followed along its vanishing outline, leaving his air bubbles to swirl and rise lazily to the surface. As he sank deeper and deeper, the light diminished and the visibility shortened. He checked his two vital references. The depth gauge read ninety feet and the orange dial on the Doxa diving watch notified him that he had been down two minutes.

The bottom gradually came into view. He automatically popped his ears for the third time and was struck by the color of the sand—a pure black. Unlike most areas of the world where the bottom sand was white, the volcanic activity of Iceland had left a carpet of soft ebony grains. He slowed his movement, spellbound by the strangeness of the dark color beneath the vast shroud of blue-green water. Visibility was about forty feet—quite good considering the depth.

Instinctively he swung around in a three-hundred-and-sixty-degree circle. Nothing was in sight. He looked up and vaguely saw a shadow pass over him. It was a small school of cod foraging near the bottom for their favorite diet of shrimp and crab. He watched a moment as they slowly slipped overhead, their slightly flattened bodies tinted a dark olive and spotted with hundreds of small brown dots. Too bad the admiral can't hook one, he thought. The smallest weighed no less than fifteen pounds.

Pitt began swimming in ever-widening circles

around the anchor line, dragging a fin in the sand to mark his trail. Underwater he often saw fantasy, at deep depths his perception was distorted, danger magnified beyond clear thinking. After five circuits he saw a dim form through the blue haze. Quickly kicking his fins, he swam toward it. Thirty seconds later his hopes were broken and discarded. The form proved to be a large jagged rock poking up from the bottom like some forgotten and crumbling outpost in the middle of a desert. Effortlessly he slipped around the current-worn sides, his mind blurred, struggling for control. This couldn't be the reading on the fathometer, he thought. The peak was too conical to match that of an aircraft fuselage.

Then he saw something lying in the sand just five feet away. The black paint on the broken and bent door blended against the black sand almost to the point of invisibility. He swam forward and turned it over, recoiling in surprise for an instant as a large lobster scurried from its new home. There were no markings anywhere on the inside paneling. Pitt had to move quickly now. The plane had to be very close, but he was due to pull the valve for his reserve air, and that only left a few minutes of extra breathing—barely enough to get him to the surface.

It didn't take him long to find it. The aircraft was resting on its belly, broken in two, evidence of the impact from the crash. His breathing became harder now, signaling him that it was time to go on reserve. He pulled the valve and headed for the top. The watery ceiling over his head slowly became brighter as he rose along with his air bubbles. At thirty feet he stopped and searched for *The Grimsi*'s keel. He stared upward at the sun to get a direction. *The Grimsi* had drifted around her anchor line on a hundred-and-eighty-degree arc so that her starboard side now faced the coast.

He pulled himself over the port freeboard and, dropping his air tank, crawled across the deck into the wheelhouse. Sandecker, without looking up, slowly placed his rod against the railing and just as slowly walked over and leaned in the doorway.

"I hope you've had better luck than I have."

"She's lying a hundred and fifty feet off the starboard beam," Pitt said. "I didn't have time to search the interior; my air was scraping bottom."

"Better get out of that suit and rest belowdecks. Your face is as blue as a windmill on a Delftware saucer."

"I'll relax as soon as we've got what we came for." Pitt started for the door.

Sandecker's eyes were set. "You're not going anywhere for the next hour and a half. We still have plenty of time. The day is young. It's senseless to overdo your physical resources. You know the repetitive dive charts as well as any diver alive. Two dives to one hundred and forty feet within thirty minutes invites a case of the bends." He paused, then drove the point home. "You've seen men scream their lungs out from the agony of pain. You know the ones who lived and the ones who were paralyzed for life. Even if I pushed this old scow to the hilt, I couldn't get you to Reykjavik before two hours. Then, add another five hours on a jet to London and the nearest decompression chamber. No way, my friend. You go below and rest up. I'll tell you when you can go down again."

"No contest, Admiral; you win." Pitt unzipped the front of his wet suit. "However, I think it would be wiser to sack out above deck so that all three of us are in view."

"Who's to see? The coast is deserted, and we haven't seen another boat since we left the harbor."

"The coast isn't deserted. We have an observer."

Sandecker turned and gazed across the water toward the cliffs. "I may be getting old, but I don't need glasses yet. I can't detect any obvious signs."

"Off to the right just beyond that rock that projects from the water."

"Can't see a thing from this distance." He stared sideways at the point Pitt described. "It'd be like looking through a keyhole and seeing another eye if I picked up the binoculars and stared back. How can you be sure?"

"There was a reflection. The sun flashed on something for a moment. Probably a pair of lenses."

"Let them gawk. If anybody should ask why only two of us were on deck, we'll say Tidi was seasick and in misery on a bunk below."

"That's as good an excuse as any," Pitt said, smiling as he headed below for a much-needed nap.

* * *

An eerie, yellow-gray light showed through the hatch when Sandecker shook Pitt awake. He woke slowly, mind blurred, more groggy from a catnap than from an eight-hour sleep. Pitt could feel the drop in the wave action; *The Grimsi* was barely rocking, even in the low even swells. There was no hint of a breeze. The air was damp and heavy.

"A change in the weather, Admiral?"

"A fog bank—rolling in from the south."

"How long?"

"Fifteen, maybe twenty minutes."

"Not much time."

"Enough . . . enough for a quick dive."

Minutes later Pitt had slipped into his gear and dropped over the side. Down again into a world where there is no sound, no wind; down where air is not known. He cleared his ears and kicked his fins hard and descended, his muscles cold and aching, his brain still sluggish from sleep.

He swam silently, effortlessly, as though suspended by a wire through the great fluid backdrop. He swam through the darkening colors, the blue-green now changing slowly to a soft gray. He swam with no sense of direction, except for what his instinct and the landmarks on the bottom told him. Then he found it.

His heart began pounding like a bass drum as he approached the plane cautiously, knowing from experience that once he entered the tangled wreckage, every movement would be a menace.

As soon as his eyes adjusted to the darkness, they met with a jumbled mess of seats, broken from their moorings on the floor, and wooden boxes floating in confusion against the ceiling. Tugging two of the boxes toward the opening, he pushed them out and watched until they lifted free on their way toward the surface. Then he spied a glove still encasing a man's hand. The body attached by a greenish arm to the hand was jammed between the seats in the lower corner of the main cabin.

Pitt pulled the corpse out and searched its clothing. He must have been the one who fired the machine gun from the doorway, Pitt reasoned. The pockets of the torn black overalls covering the remains held nothing but a screwdriver.

Pitt shoved the screwdriver under his weightbelt then, half swimming, half gliding, he entered the cockpit. Except for a broken windshield on the copilot's side, the heart of the aircraft appeared empty and undamaged. But then he happened to look up at his air bubbles rising to the overhead panel and traveling like a silver snake in search of an escape exit. They eventually ran together and clustered in one corner, encircling another corpse.

The dead pilot wore the same type of black overalls. A quick search revealed nothing; the pockets were empty. Pitt pushed the body upward out of the way. He glanced at his Doxa watch. He had only been down for nine minutes, not the ninety his imagination suggested. There was little time left. Quickly he groped around the small enclosure, looking for a log book, a maintenance or check-out list, anything with printing on it. The cockpit kept its secret well.

There was no record of any kind. Not even a sticker with the aircraft's call letters adhering to the face of the radio transmitter.

The open water was darker when he emerged from the plane than when he had entered. After checking the tail section, he kicked over to the starboard engine. No hope here; it was almost totally buried in the bottom silt. He got lucky on the port engine. He discovered the area where the identification plate should have been. It was gone. Only the four little brass screws that once held it remained, neatly set in their threads.

Pitt slammed his fist against the casing in frustration. He knew all identifying marks on instruments, electrical components, and other mechanical units on the plane would be erased. In spite of the near freezing water, trickles of sweat rolled down his face under the mask. His mind was turning aimlessly, posing problems and questions. Then, as he was about to head toward the surface, he threw a last quick look down. On the end section of the housing where the hydraulic tubing had pulled from its connection, Pitt spotted a small marking: two roughly gouged letters in the metal—SC. Taking the screwdriver from his weightbelt, he etched his initials next to the other marking. The depth of his DP matched that of the SC.

Okay. No sense in hanging around, he reasoned. His air was becoming difficult to inhale—the signal that his tank was getting low. He pulled his reserve valve and moved upward.

Pitt arched on his back at fifty feet, looking directly up at where the surface should have been, trying to get his bearings in relation to *The Grimsi*. The light was equal in all directions, only his ascending bubbles indicated the direction of his native element. It slowly began to get lighter, but it was still much darker than when he dropped off *The Grimsi*'s side. Pitt's anxious head broke water, to be engulfed by a thick cloak of fog.

Pitt unshouldered his airtank harness, tied it to his already unhooked weightbelt, and let them fall together to the bottom. Now he could float comfortably, thanks to the buoyancy of his rubber wet suit. He lay quietly, barely breathing, listening for a sound through the dense gray blanket. At first he could hear only the water lapping around his body. Then his ears picked up a faint gravelly voice . . . a voice singing a flat version of "My Bonnie Lies over the Ocean." Pitt cupped his ears, amplifying the sound, determining the direction. He struck out with an easy energy-saving breast stroke for fifty feet and then stopped. The offkey singing had increased in volume. Five minutes later he touched the seaworn hull of *The Grimsi* and pulled himself on board.

"Have a nice swim?" Sandecker asked conversationally.

"Hardly enjoyable and barely profitable." Pitt unzipped the wet suit top. He grinned at the admiral. "Funny thing. I could swear I heard a foghorn."

"That was no foghorn. That was a former baritone of the Annapolis Glee Club."

"You were never in better voice, Admiral." Pitt looked Sandecker in the eye. "Thanks."

Sandecker smiled. "Don't thank me, thank Tidi. She had to sit through ten choruses."

She materialized out of the mist and hugged him. "Thank goodness you're safe."

"Did you find anything of value?" Sandecker asked.

"Two bodies and little else. Somebody went to a lot of work to remove the plane's identification. Every serial number on every piece of equipment had been removed before the crash. The only markings were two letters scratched on the nose gear's hydraulic cylinder." He gratefully accepted a towel from Tidi. "The boxes I sent up. Did you retrieve them?"

"It wasn't easy," Sandecker said. "They broke surface about forty feet away. Twenty tries later—I haven't cast with a pole in years—I managed to hook and reel them in."

"You opened them?" Pitt probed.

"Yes. They're miniature models of buildings . . . like dollhouses."

Pitt straightened. "Dollhouses? You mean three-dimensional architectural exhibits?"

"Call them what you want. The detail on each structure is amazing. They even break away by floors so you can study the interior."

"Let's take a look."

"We carried them to the galley," Sandecker said. "It's as good a place as any to get you into some dry clothes and a cup of hot cocoa into your stomach."

In the galley Sandecker lifted the boxes onto the table and pulled off the lids. "OK, here they are, including furniture and draperies."

Pitt looked into the first box. "No indications of water damage."

"They were watertight," Sandecker offered. "Each packed so carefully the crash left them entirely intact."

To say the models were simply masterpieces of diminutive art would have been a gross understatement. The admiral was right. The detail was amazing. Every brick, every windowpane, was precise in scale and placement. Pitt lifted off the roof. He had seen model exhibits before in museums, but never workmanship like this. Nothing had been overlooked. Paintings on the walls were exacting in color and design. The furniture had tiny designs printed on the fabric. Telephones on desks had receivers that could be picked up, connected to wires that led into the walls. As a crowning touch, the bathrooms even possessed toilet paper rolls that unraveled to the touch. The first model building consisted of four floors and a basement. Pitt carefully lifted them off one at a time, studied the contents and just as carefully replaced them. Then he inspected the second model.

"I know this one," Pitt said quietly.

Sandecker looked up. "Are you sure?"

"Positive. It's pink. You don't often forget a structure built of pink marble. It was about six years ago when I entered those walls. My father was on an economic survey mission for the President, conferring with the heads of finance of Latin American governments. I took a thirty-day leave from the Air Force and acted as his aide and pilot during the trip."

"Where is it located?" Tidi asked.

"In El Salvador. This model is a perfect scaled-down replica of the Dominican Republic capitol building." He gestured toward the first model. "Judging from the design, the other model also represents the legislative offices of another South or Central American country."

"Great," Sandecker said unenthusiastically. "We've come up with a character who collects miniature capitols."

"It doesn't tell us a lot." Tidi handed Pitt a cup of cocoa and he sipped it thoughtfully. "Except that the black jet was doing double duty."

Sandecker met his gaze. "You mean it was delivering these models when it changed course to shoot down you and Hunnewell?"

"Exactly. One of Rondheim's fishing trawlers probably spotted our helicopter approaching Iceland and diverted the jet by radio so it would be waiting for us when we reached the coast."

"Why Rondheim? I see nothing tangible that ties him in with any of this?"

Pitt shrugged. "I admit I'm groping. And, at that, I'm not completely sold on implicating Rondheim myself. He's like the butler in an old movie mystery. Every piece of circumstantial evidence, every finger of doubt, points to him, making him the most obvious suspect. But in the end, our friendly butler turns out to be an undercover policeman and the least obvious character turns out to be the guilty party."

Pitt suddenly stiffened, held up a hand for silence. He stepped to the wheelhouse doorway and listened intently. It was very faint, but it was there. Through the blanket of mist it came as a steady drone: the sound of an engine running at very high rpm's.

7

"Do you hear it, Admiral?"

"I hear it." Sandecker was at his shoulder. "About three miles, coming fast." He concentrated for a few seconds. "I make it dead ahead."

Pitt nodded. "Coming straight toward us." He stared unseeing into the fog. "Sounds strange, almost like the whine of an aircraft engine. They must have radar. No helmsman with half a brain would run at full speed in this weather."

"A hydrofoil. Is that it?" Sandecker asked slowly.

"Exactly," Pitt answered. "Which means their top speed could be anywhere between forty-five and sixty knots."

"Not good," Sandecker said quietly.

"Not bad either," Pitt returned. "We've got at least two advantages in our favor." Quickly he outlined his plan.

The unseen boat was almost upon them, the roar of its engine dying to a muted throb as the helmsman eased back the throttles in preparation for coming alongside *The Grimsi*. From where he lay on the bow, clenching and unclenching his hands around the handle of the *Grimsi*'s fire ax, Pitt could hear the hull splash into the waves as the diminishing speed pushed the hydrofoil deeper in the water. He raised himself carefully, narrowing his eyes and trying vainly to pierce the heavy fog for a sign of movement. The area round the bow was in near darkness. Visibility was no more than twenty feet.

Then a shadowy bulk slowly eased into view, showing its port bow. Pitt could barely make out several dim forms standing on the forward deck, a glow behind them that Pitt knew would be the wheelhouse. The large gray form arose menacingly and towered above *The Grimsi;* the stranger had a length of a hundred feet or better, Pitt guessed. He could see the other men clearly now, leaning over the bulwarks, saying nothing, crouched as if ready to jump. The automatic rifles in their hands told Pitt all he needed to know.

Coolly and precisely, no more than eight feet from the gun barrels on the specter ship, Pitt made three movements so rapidly they almost seemed simultaneous. Swinging the ax head sideways, he brought the flat face down loudly on an iron capstan—the signal to Sandecker. Then in the same swinging motion he hurled the ax through the air and saw it hit a man who was in the act of jumping down on *The Grimsi*'s deck. They met in midair, a ghastly scream reaching from the man's throat as he and the ax fell against the railing. He hung there for an instant, the bloodless nails of one hand clenched over the wooden molding and then dropped into the gray water. Even before the sea closed over the man's head, Pitt had hurled himself on the worn planks of the deck, and *The Grimsi* leaped ahead like a frightened impala, chased by a storm of shells that swept across the deck and into the wheelhouse before the old boat had vanished into the mist.

Staying below the gunwale, Pitt crawled aft and across the threshold of the wheelhouse doorway. The floor was littered with glass and wood splinters.

"Any hits?" Sandecker asked, his voice hardly audible above the exhaust of the Sterling engines.

"No holes in me. The problem now is to prevent a repeat performance."

"It won't be easy. We're running blind. Their radar knows our every move. Our biggest fear is ramming. With a ten-to-twenty-knot edge they're an odds-on favorite to win at blindman's bluff. I can't avoid the inevitable. If their helmsman is halfway on the dime, he'll use his superior speed to pass and then cut a ninety-degree angle and catch us amidships."

Pitt considered a moment. "This will give us an opportunity to use one of our two advantages."

Sandecker looked at him. "I can't think of one, much less two."

"A hydrofoil boat depends on its high speed to sustain its weight. The foils travel through the water the same as the wings of an aircraft travel through air. Its greatest asset is speed, but its greatest limitation is maneuverability. In simple English, a hydrofoil can't turn to save itself."

"And we can. Is that it?" Sandecker probed.

"The Grimsi can cut two circles inside their one."

Sandecker lifted his hands from the spokes of the wheel and flexed his fingers. "Sounds great as far as it goes, except we won't know when they start their arc."

Pitt sighed. "We listen."

Sandecker looked at him. "Shut down our engines?"

Pitt nodded.

Sandecker cast a searching stare at the tall man standing in the doorway. He could see that the eyes were determined and the chin set.

"You mentioned two advantages."

"The unexpected," Pitt said quietly. "We know what they're out to do. They may have radar, but they can't read our minds. That is our second and most important advantage—the unexpected move."

Pitt looked at his Doxa watch. One-thirty, still early in the afternoon. Sandecker had cut the engines, and Pitt had to fight to stay alert—the sudden silence and the calm of the fog began a creeping course to dull his mind. Above, the sun was a faded white disc that brightened and dimmed as the uneven layers of mist rolled overhead. He sat there on the forward hatch cover, waiting until his hearing picked up the engines of the hydroplane. He didn't have to wait long. He soon tuned in the steady beat of the hydroplane as the explosions through its exhaust manifolds increased in volume.

Pitt rechecked the containers lying in a neat row beside him for perhaps the tenth time. It had to be the poorest excuse for an arsenal ever concocted, he mused. One of the containers was a gallon glass jar Tidi had scrounged from the galley. The other three were battered and rusty gas cans in various sizes that Pitt had found in a locker aft of the engine room. Except for their contents, the cloth wicks protruding from the cap openings and the holes punched through the top of the cans, the four vessels had little in common.

The hydroplane was close now—very close. Pitt turned to the wheelhouse and shouted, "Now!" Then he lit the wick of the glass jar with his lighter and braced himself for the sudden surge of acceleration he hoped would come.

Sandecker pushed the starter button. The 420-hp Sterlings coughed once, twice, then burst into rpm's with a roar. He swung the wheel over to starboard hard and jammed the throttles forward. *The Grimsi* took off over the water like a racehorse leaving the starting gate. The admiral held on grimly, clutching the wheel and half expecting to collide with the hydroplane bow on. Then suddenly as a spoke flew off the wheel and clattered against the compass, he became aware that bullets were striking the wheelhouse. He could still see nothing, but he knew the crew of the hydroplane were firing blindly through the fog, guided only by the commands of the radar operator.

To Pitt the tension was unbearable. His gaze alternated from the wall of fog in front of the bow to the jar in his hand. The flame on the wick was getting dangerously close to the tapered neck and the gasoline sloshing behind the glass. Five seconds, no more, then he would have to heave the jar over the side. He began counting. Five came and went. Six, seven. He cocked his arm. Eight. Then the hydroplane leaped from the mist on an opposite course, passing no more than ten feet from *The Grimsi*'s railing. Pitt hurled the jar.

A thunderous shock wave knocked Pitt to the deck and blew out what glass was left in the windows around Sandecker. The hydroplane had erupted in a volcanic roar of fire and flaming debris, instantly becoming a blazing inferno from end to end.

Pitt pushed himself shakily to his feet and stared incredulously at the hydroplane. What had once been a superbly designed boat was now a shambles and burning furiously down to the water's edge. He staggered to the wheelhouse—his sense of balance temporarily crippled by the ringing in his ears from the concussion—as Sandecker slowed *The Grimsi* and drifted past the fiery wreck.

"See any survivors?" Sandecker asked. He had a thin slice on one cheek that trickled blood.

Pitt shook his head. "They've had it," he said. "Even if any of the crew made it to the water alive, they'd die of exposure before we could find them in this soup."

Tidi entered the wheelhouse, one hand nursing a purplish bruise on her forehead, her expression one of total bewilderment. "What . . . what happened?" was all she could stammer.

"It wasn't the fuel tanks," Sandecker said. "Of that much I'm certain."

"I agree," Pitt said grimly. "They must have had explosives lying abovedecks that got in the way of my last homemade firebomb."

The hydroplane was going down by the stern, sinking rapidly. The sea crowded over the gunwales and swamped the flames, hissing in a cloud of steam, and the hydroplane was gone. It was as though the boat had been nothing but a nebulous nightmare that vanished with the passing of night.

Pitt pulled his mind back to practical reality. "No sense in hanging around. I suggest we head back to Reykjavik as fast as we dare through this fog. The quicker and the farther we high tail it out of this area before the weather clears, the better for all concerned."

Three hours later and twenty miles southwest of Reykjavik they rounded the tip of the Keflavik peninsula and broke out of the fog. Iceland's seemingly eternal sun greeted them in a dazzling brilliance.

It was four o'clock when they tied up to the Fyrie dock. The ramp was deserted, the dockmaster and the guard obvious by their absence. Pitt and

Sandecker weren't fooled. They knew their every move had been studied the second *The Grimsi* rounded the harbor breakwater.

Before he followed Tidi and Sandecker away from the forlorn and battered little boat, Pitt left a note on the helm.

SORRY ABOUT THE MESS. WE WERE AT-
TACKED BY A SWARM OF RED-NECKED
FUZZWORTS. PUT THE REPAIRS ON
OUR TAB.

He signed it *Admiral James Sandecker.*

Twenty minutes later they reached the consulate. The young staff members who played such profes-sional roles as bait fishermen beat them by five min-utes and had already locked the two models away in the consul's vault. Sandecker thanked them warmly and promised to replace the diving gear Pitt had been forced to jettison with the best that U.S. Divers manufactured.

Pitt then quickly showered and changed clothes and took a taxi to the airport at Keflavik.

"Do you wish to go to the main terminal, sir?" the driver asked.

"No, the maintenance hangars."

"Sorry, sir. They are on the edge of the field be-yond the passenger terminal. Only authorized cars are permitted on the flight line."

There was something about the cab driver's ac-cent that intrigued Pitt. Then it came to him. There was an unmistakable American midwestern quality about it.

"Let's give it a try, shall we?"

The driver shrugged and pulled the cab up to the flight line gate and stopped where a tall, thin, gray-haired man in a blue uniform stepped from a guard shack. He touched his fingers to his cap brim in a friendly salute. Pitt rolled down the window, leaned out, and showed his Air Force I.D.

"Major Dirk Pitt," he snapped in an official tone, introducing himself. "I'm on urgent business for the United States government and must get to the commercial maintenance hangar for nonscheduled aircraft."

The guard looked at him blankly until he finished and then, smiling dumbly, shrugged.

The cab driver stepped from behind the steering wheel. "He doesn't understand English, Major. Allow me to translate for you."

Without waiting for an acknowledgment, the driver put an arm around the guard and gently walked him away from the car toward the gate, talking rapidly but gesturing gracefully as he rattled off a flow of words in Icelandic. It was the first chance that Pitt had a good look at his helpmate.

The driver was medium height, just under six foot, not more than twenty-six or twenty-seven years old, with straw-colored hair and the light skin that usually goes with it.

Finally the two men broke out laughing and shook hands. Then the driver climbed back behind the wheel and winked at Pitt as the still-smiling guard opened the gate and waved them through.

Pitt said, "You seem to have a way with security guards."

"A necessity of the trade. A cab driver wouldn't be worth his salt if he couldn't talk his way past a gate guard or a policeman on a barricaded street."

"It's apparent you've mastered the knack."

"I work at it . . . Any particular hangar, sir? There are several, one for every major airline."

"General maintenance—the one that handles transient nonscheduled aircraft."

The glare of the sun bounced off the white cement taxiway and made Pitt squint. He slipped a pair of sunglasses from a breast pocket and put them on. Several huge jetliners were parked in even rows, displaying the emblems and color schemes of their airlines, while crews of white-coveralled mechanics buried themselves under engine cowlings and crawled over the wings with fuel hoses. On the other side of the field, a good two miles away, Pitt could make out aircraft of the U.S. Air Force, undoubtedly going through the same rituals.

"Here we are," the driver announced. "Permit me to offer you my services as a translator."

"That won't be necessary. Keep the meter running. I'll only be a few minutes."

Pitt got out and walked through the side door of the hangar, a sterile giant of a building that covered nearly two acres. Five small private planes were scattered around the floor like a handful of spectators in an otherwise empty auditorium. But it was the sixth that caught Pitt's eye. It was an old Ford tri-motor known as the Tin Goose. The corrugated aluminum skin that covered the framework and the three motors, one perched on the nose directly in front of the cockpit, the other two suspended in space by an ungainly network of wires and struts, combined to make it look to the unknowing eye a thing too awkward to fly with any degree of control or, for that matter, lift its wheels from the ground. But the old pioneering pilots swore by it. Pitt patted the ancient washboard sides, idly wished he could test-fly it someday, and then walked on toward the offices in the rear of the hangar.

He opened a door and moved into what appeared to be a combination locker room and rest area. He stood there a moment looking at a group of five men dressed in white coveralls, some spotlessly clean, others decorated with heavy splotches of black oil. Pitt sauntered easily toward them, smiling.

"Pardon me, gentlemen, any of you speak English?"

A shaggy, long-haired mechanic looked up and drawled, "Yeah, I speak American if that'll do."

"That will do fine," Pitt laughed. "I'm looking for a man with the initials S.C. He's probably a hydraulic specialist."

The mechanic eyed him uneasily. "Who wants to know?"

Pitt forced a friendly smile and pulled out his I.D. again.

"Pitt, Major Dirk Pitt."

"Ya got your man, Major." The voice reached from somewhere deep in Oklahoma. "Sam . . . Sam Cashman," he said. "Sergeant. Air Force 19385628."

"I wonder if you would answer a few simple questions." Pitt stared Cashman in the eye and smiled warmly. "Will you help me?"

Cashman extended his hand. "Ask away, Major."

Pitt returned Cashman's grip. "First question: do you usually scratch your initials in the equipment you repair?"

"Yeah, it's kind of a trademark, ya might say. Ah do good work an ah'm proud of it. Serves a purpose too. If ah work on the hydraulic system of an aircraft and it comes back with a malfunction, ah know the trouble lays where ah didn't work. It saves a lot of time."

"Have you ever repaired the nose gear of a twelve-passenger British jet?"

Cashman thought for a moment. "Yeah, about a month ago. One of those new executive twin turbine Loreleis—a great machine."

"Was it painted black?"

"Ah couldn't see paint markins. It was dark, about one-thirty in the mornin' when ah got the call." He shook his head. "Wasn't black, though. Ah'm positive."

"Any distinguishing features or anything unusual about the repair that you can recall?"

Cashman laughed. "The only distinguishin' features were the two weirdos who were flyin' it. These guys were in a terrible hurry. Kept standin' around tryin' to push me. Seems they made a rough landin' somewhere and busted a seal in the shock cylinder."

"Did you get a look inside?"

"Oh no, you'd have thought they had the President on board the way they guarded the loadin' door."

"Any idea where they came from or where they were headed?"

"No way, they were sure tight-lipped. Talked about nothin' but the repair. Must have been on a local flight though. They didn't refuel. You ain't flyin' far in a Lorelei—not from Iceland anyhow—without full tanks."

"The pilot must have signed a maintenance order."

"Nope. He refused. Said he was behind schedule and would catch me next time. Paid me though. Twice what the job was worth." Cashman was silent for a moment. He tried to read something in the man standing before him, but Pitt's face was as impenetrable as a granite statue. "What's behind these questions, Major? Mind lettin' me in on your secret?"

"No secret," Pitt said slowly. "A Lorelei crashed a couple of days ago and nothing except a portion of the nose gear was left to identify. I'm trying to trace it, that's all."

"Wasn't it reported as missin'?"

"I wouldn't be here if it was."

"Ah knew there was something fishy about them guys. That's why ah went ahead and filled out a maintenance report."

Pitt leaned over, his eyes boring into Cashman's.

"What good was a report if you couldn't identify the aircraft?"

A shrewd smile split Cashman's lips. "Ah may be a country boy, but ah know a thing or two." He stood up and tilted his head toward a side door. "Major, ah'm gonna make your day."

He led Pitt into a small dingy office furnished with only a battered desk that was decorated with at least fifty cigarette burn marks, two equally battered chairs and a huge metal filing cabinet. Cashman walked straight to the cabinet and pulled out a drawer, rummaged for a moment, found what he was looking for, and handed Pitt a folder soiled with greasy fingerprints.

"Ah wasn't kiddin' ya, Major, when ah said it was too dark to make out any paint markin's. Near as ah could tell, the plane had never been touched by a brush or spray gun. The aluminum skin was as shiny as the day it left the factory."

Pitt opened the folder and scanned the maintenance report. Cashman's handwriting left much to be desired, but there was no mistaking the notation under AIRCRAFT IDENTIFICATION: Lorelei Mark VIII-B1608.

"How did you get it?" Pitt asked.

"Compliments of an inspector at the Lorelei factory," Cashman answered, sitting on a corner of the desk. "After replacin' the seal on the nose gear, ah took a flashlight and checked out the main landin' gear for damage or leakage, and there it was, stuck away under the right strut as pretty as you please. A green tag sayin' that this here aircraft's landin' gear had been examined and okayed by master inspector Clarence Devonshire of Lorelei Aircraft Limited. The plane's serial number was typed on the tag."

Pitt threw the folder on the desk. "Sergeant Cashman!" he snapped.

Stunned at the brusque tone, Cashman jumped erect. "Sir?"

"Your squadron!"

"Eighty-seventh Air Transport Squadron, sir."

"Good enough." Pitt's cold expression slowly worked into a huge grin and he slapped Cashman on the shoulder. "You're absolutely right, Sam. You truly made my day."

"Wish ah could say the same," Cashman sighed, visibly relieved. "Why'd ya want mah squadron?"

"So I'd know where to send a nice big juicy steak dinner as a thank-you."

A look of wonder suddenly came over Cashman's face. "Major, you're sumthin' else. Ya know that?"

"I try. By the way, have you ever seen this before?" He handed Cashman the screwdriver he'd found on the black Lorelei.

"Waal, waal, fancy that. Believe it or not, Major, this here screwtwister is mine. Bought it through the catalog of a tool specialty house in Chicago. It's the only one of its kind on the island. Where'd you come across it?"

"In the wreck."

"So that's where it went," he said angrily. "Those creeps stole it. Ah should a known they were up to sumthin' illegal. Ya just tell me when their trial is, and ah'll be happier than a rejected hog at a packin' plant to testify against them."

"Save your leave time for a worthwhile escapade. Your friends won't be showing for a trial. They bought the farm."

"Killed in the wreck?" It was more statement than question.

Pitt nodded.

"Ah suppose ah could go on about crime not payin', but why bother. If they had it comin', they had it comin'. That's all there is to it."

"As a philosopher, you make a great hydraulic specialist, Sam." Pitt shook Cashman's hand once more. "Good-by and thank you. I'm grateful for your help."

"Glad to do it, Major. Here, keep the screwdriver for a souvenir. Already ordered a new one, so won't be needin' it."

"Thanks again." Pitt shoved the screwdriver back in his pocket, turned and left the office.

8

Pitt relaxed in the cab. Obtaining the mysterious black jet's serial number had been a shot in the dark that paid off. He really hadn't expected to find out anything. Staring through the window at the passing green pastures, he saw nothing with his eyes, idly wondering if the plane could now be tied directly to Rondheim. His mind was still wandering over the possibility when he had the vague impression that the countryside looked different than before. The fields were empty of cattle and ponies, the rolling hills flattened into a vast carpet of uneven tundra. He swung around and gazed out the other window; the sea was not where it should have been; instead, it lay to the rear of the cab, slowly disappearing over a long, low rise in the road. He leaned over the front seat.

"Do you have a date with the farmer's daughter or are you taking the scenic route to run up the meter?"

The driver applied pressure to the brake and slowed the cab, stopping at the side of the road. "Privacy is the word, Major. Merely a slight detour so we can have a little chat—"

The driver's voice froze into nothingness, and for good reason. Pitt had the tip of the screwdriver in the cavity of his ear.

"Keep your hands on the wheel and get this hack back on the road to Reykjavik," Pitt said quietly, "or your right ear will get screwed into your left."

Pitt watched the driver's face closely in the rearview mirror, studying the blue eyes, knowing they would signal any sudden attempt at resistance. No shadow of an expression touched the boyish features, not even a flicker of fear. Then slowly, very slowly, the face in the mirror began to smile, the smile transforming into a genuine laugh.

"Major Pitt, you are a very suspicious man."

"If you had three attempts on your life in the last three days, you'd develop a suspicious nature too."

The laugh stopped abruptly and the bush brows bunched together. "Three attempts? I'm aware of only two—"

Pitt cut him off by pushing the screwdriver another eighth of an inch deeper. "You're a lucky man, friend. I could try and make you contribute a few choice items about your boss and his operation. Instead of Reykjavik, suppose you drive nice and easy back to Keflavik, only this time to the United States Air Force side of the field.

"That might prove embarrassing."

"That's your problem."

The smile was back in the rearview mirror. "Not entirely, Major. It would, indeed, be a moment worth remembering to see your face when you discover you brought in an N.I.A. agent for questioning."

Pitt's pressure on the screwdriver didn't relax. "Very second-rate," he said. "I'd expect a better story from a high school freshman caught smoking in the boy's room."

"Admiral Sandecker said you wouldn't be an easy man to talk to."

Pitt hoped the look of surprise was not visible to the driver. "When did you talk to the admiral?"

"In his office at NUMA headquarters."

The driver's answer tallied with what Pitt knew: the N.I.A. had not contacted Sandecker since he had arrived in Iceland. Pitt glanced around the car. There was no sign of life, no sign of an ambush by possible accomplices. He started to relax, caught himself, and then clenched the screwdriver until his fingers ached.

"Okay, be my guest," Pitt said casually. Describe him. Size, hair, mannerisms, layout of his office—everything."

The driver needed no further coaxing. He talked for several minutes and ended up by mentioning a few of Sandecker's pet slang terms.

"Your memory is good—nearly letter-perfect."

"I have a photographic memory, Major. Take a rundown of yourself for example: Major Dirk Eric Pitt. Born exactly thirty-two years, four months and twelve days ago at the Hoag Hospital in Newport Beach, California. Mother's name Barbara, father George Pitt, senior United States Senator from your home state. No sense in going on about your three rows of combat ribbons which you never wear. If you like, I can give you a detailed hour-by-hour account of your actions since you left Washington."

Pitt released the screwdriver and put it back in his pocket. "That will do. I'm impressed, of course, Mr.—ah—"

"Lillie. Jerome P. Lillie the Fourth. I'm your contact."

"Jerome P.—" Pitt made a good try but couldn't suppress an incredulous laugh. "You've got to be kidding."

Lillie gestured helplessly. "It's a last name, not a first name. I can see you're going to be a hard man to get along with," Lillie moaned.

"Not really. You couldn't possibly be one of the bad guys and come up with a story that wild."

"Your trust is warranted, Major. I told you the truth."

"You offered to give me a detailed, hour-by-hour account of my actions since I left Washington."

"Nobody's perfect, Major. I admit I lost you for two hours today."

Pitt did some fast mental arithmetic. "Where were you around noon?"

"On the southern shore of the island."

"Doing what?"

Lillie turned away and looked across the barren

fields, his face empty of all expression. "At exactly ten minutes after twelve this afternoon I was knocking a man unconscious."

"Then there were two of you keeping an eye on *The Grimsi?*"

"The Grimsi? Ah, of course—the name of your old boat. Yes, I stumbled into the other guy quite by accident. After you and the admiral and Miss Royal took off toward the southeast, I had a hunch your anchor would drop in the area where you and Dr. Hunnewell crashed."

"Then the glint I saw from the boat was from you."

"If the sun caught the binoculars right, a visible flash would be the obvious giveaway."

Pitt was silent for a moment. "Too bad you didn't get to him five minutes sooner."

"Why is that?"

"He'd already radioed our position so his buddies could close in for the kill."

Lillie stared at Pitt questioningly.

"For what purpose? Merely to steal a few sketches or a bucket of fish?"

"Something much more important. A jet aircraft."

"I know. Your mysterious black jet. The thought had occurred that you might go looking for it when I guessed your destination, but your report failed to pinpoint the exact—"

Pitt interrupted, his voice deceptively friendly. "I know for certain that Admiral Sandecker has had no contact with you or your agency since he left Washington. He and I are the only ones who know what's in that report . . ." Pitt paused, suddenly remembering. "Except—"

"Except the secretary at the consulate who typed it," Lillie finished, smiling. "My compliments, your commentary was well written." Lillie didn't bother to explain how the consulate secretary passed him a copy and Pitt didn't bother to ask him. "Tell me, Major, how do you go about dredging for a sunken aircraft with nothing but a sketch pad and a fishing pole?"

"Your victim knew the answer. He detected my air bubbles through his telescope."

Lillie's eyes narrowed. "You had diving equipment?" he asked flatly. "How? I watched you leave the dock and saw nothing. I studied you and the admiral from the shore and neither of you left the deck for more than three minutes. After that I lost visibility when the fog rolled in."

"The N.I.A. doesn't have a monopoly on sneaky, underhanded plots," Pitt said, shooting Lillie down in flames. "Let's make ourselves comfortable and I'll tell you about another ordinary garden variety day in the life of Dirk Pitt."

So Pitt slouched in the rear seat with his feet propped on the backrest of the front and told Lillie what had happened from the time *The Grimsi* left the Fyrie dock until it had returned. He told what he knew for certain and what he didn't, everything, that is, except for one little indefinable thought that kept itching in his mind—a thought that concerned Kirsti Fyrie.

* * *

"So you've selected Oskar Rondheim as your villain," Lillie murmured. "You haven't convinced me with any solid proof."

"I agree, it's all circumstantial," Pitt said. "Rondheim has the most to gain. Therefore, Rondheim has the motive. He murdered to get his hands on the undersea probe and he's murdered to cover his tracks."

"You'll have to do better than that."

Pitt looked at Lillie. "Okay, come up with a better one."

"Until I receive orders to the contrary, I can't fully brief an outsider on all the details of the operation I'm part of." Lillie's voice carried an official tone that didn't quite come off. "I can, however, acknowledge your conclusions. You are quite correct in everything you've said. Beyond that there is little I can officially tell you that you don't already know."

"Since we've become such close friends," Pitt said, grinning, "why don't you call me Dirk?"

"Have it your way. But don't you dare call me Jerome—it's Jerry." He held out his hand. "Okay, partner. Don't make me sorry I took you into the firm."

Pitt returned the grip. "Stick with the kid here and you'll go places."

"That's what I'm afraid of." Lillie sighed and gazed over the barren countryside for a moment as if weighing the turn of events. Finally he broke his thoughts and looked at his watch. "We'd better head back to Reykjavik. No thanks to you, I've got a busy night ahead of me."

"What's on your agenda?"

"First, I want to contact headquarters as soon as possible and pass on the serial number of the black jet. With a bit of luck they should be able to run a make and have the owner's name back to us by morning. For your sake, after all the trouble you went to, I hope it provides an important lead. Second, I'm going to poke around and see where that hydroplane was moored. Somebody has got to know something. You can't keep a craft like that a secret on an island this small. And third, the two scaled replicas of South American capitol buildings. I'm afraid you threw us a weird twist when you fished them from the briny deep. They must have a functional purpose. They may be vital to whoever built them, or they may not. Just to play safe, I'd better request Washington to fly in an expert on miniatures and have every square inch of those models thoroughly examined."

"Efficient, industrious, professional. Keep it up. I may slowly become impressed."

"I'll try to do my best," Lillie said sarcastically.

"Would you like an extra hand?" Pitt asked. "I'm free for the evening."

Lillie smiled a smile that made Pitt feel a twinge of uneasiness. "Your plans are already made, Dirk. I wish I could trade places with you, but duty calls."

"I'm afraid to ask what's on your mind," Pitt said dryly.

"A party, you lucky dog. You're going to a poetry reading party."

"You've got to be kidding."

"No, I'm serious. By special invitation from Oskar Rondheim himself. Though I suspect it was Miss Fyrie's idea."

Pitt's eyebrows came together over his penetrating green eyes. "How do you know this? How *could* you know this? No invitation arrived before you picked me up at the consulate."

"A trade secret. We *do* manage to pull a rabbit out of the hat occasionally."

"Okay, I'll concede a point and stick a gold star on your chart for the day." It was beginning to get chilly so Pitt rolled up his window. "A poetry reading," he said. "That ought to be a winner."

101

9

The entire block in front of the ornate grille doors of Oskar Rondheim's house was lined with limousines representing every expensive auto manufacturer of every country: Rolls-Royce, Lincoln, Mercedes-Benz, Cadillac. Even a Russian-built Zis stood temporarily in the circular driveway, unloading its cargo of formally dressed passengers.

Beyond the entryway, eighty to ninety guests drifted in and out of the main salon and the terrace, conversing in a spectrum of different languages. The midnight sun, which had been hidden off and on by a stray cloud, shone brightly through the windows even though it was just past nine o'clock in the evening. At the far end of the great salon, Kirsti Fyrie and Oskar Rondheim anchored the receiving line under a massive crest bearing the red albatross and greeted each arriving guest.

Pitt approached the line. "Good evening, Miss Fyrie . . . Mr. Rondheim. How good of you to invite me. Poetry readings are absolutely my favorite soirees."

Kirsti gazed at Pitt, fascinated. She said huskily: "Oskar and I are happy you could come."

"Yes, it's good to see you again, Major," Rondheim added.

To Pitt's extreme pleasure, Rondheim visibly forced himself to smile courteously. "We had hoped Admiral Sandecker and Miss Royal might also attend."

"Miss Royal will be along shortly," Pitt said, staring across the room. "But I'm afraid the admiral isn't feeling well. He decided to retire early. Poor fellow, I can't blame him after what happened this afternoon."

"Nothing serious, I hope." Rondheim's voice betrayed a lack of concern for Sandecker's health that was as obvious as his sudden interest in the reason behind the admiral's incapacity.

"Fortunately, no. The admiral only suffered a few cuts and bruises."

"An accident?" Kirsti asked.

"Dreadful, simply dreadful," Pitt said dramatically. "After you were so kind to offer us the loan of a boat, we cruised to the south side of the island where I sketched the coastline while the admiral fished. About one o'clock we found ourselves enveloped by a nasty fog. Just as we were about to return to Reykjavik, a horrible explosion occurred somewhere in the mist. The blast blew out the windows in the wheelhouse, causing a few small cuts about the admiral's head."

"An explosion?" Rondheim's voice was low and hoarse. "Do you have any idea as to the cause?"

"Afraid I haven't," Pitt said. "Couldn't see a thing. We investigated, of course, but with visibility no more than twenty feet, we found nothing."

Rondheim's face was expressionless. "Very strange. You are sure you saw nothing, Major?"

"Absolutely," Pitt said. "You're probably thinking along the same lines as Admiral Sandecker. A ship might have hit an old World War Two mine or possibly a fire broke out and touched off its fuel tanks. We notified the local coastal patrol. They have nothing to do now but wait and see what vessel is reported as missing. All in all a terrifying experience—" Pitt broke off as Tidi approached. "Ah, Tidi, here you are."

Rondheim turned on the smile again. "Miss Royal." He bowed and kissed her hand. "Major Pitt has been telling us of your harrowing experience this afternoon."

"I missed most of it, I'm afraid. The blast knocked me against a cupboard in the galley." She touched a small swelling on her forehead, the purplish bruise neatly covered by makeup. "I was pretty much out of it for the next hour and a half."

"I think it's time we mingled," Pitt said, taking her by the arm and whisking her off toward the punch bowl.

He passed her a cup of punch and they helped themselves to the hors d'oeuvres. Pitt had to fight from yawning as he and Tidi drifted from one group to another. An experienced party-goer, Pitt usually mixed with ease, but this time he couldn't seem to make a beachhead. There was an odd atmosphere about this function. He couldn't put his finger on it, yet there was something definitely out of place. Then suddenly he had it. He bent down and whispered in Tidi's ear.

"Do you get the feeling we're not welcome here?"

Tidi looked at him curiously. "No, everyone seems friendly enough."

"Sure, they're sociable and polite, but it's forced."

She looked up at Pitt with a sly smile. "You're just nervous because you're way out of your league."

He smiled back. "Care for an explanation?"

"See those two men over there?" She nodded her head sideways to her right. "Standing by the piano?"

Pitt casually rolled a slow glance in the direction Tidi indicated. A small, rotund, lively little man with a bald head was gesturing animatedly as he spoke in rapid bursts into a wiry, thick white beard no more than ten inches from his nose. The beard belonged to a thin, distinguished-looking man with silver hair that fell well below his collar, giving him the appearance of a Harvard professor. Pitt turned back to Tidi and shrugged.

"So?"

"You don't recognize them?"

"Should I?"

Her eyes flew wide in surprise. "Only two of the richest men in the world. The bald-headed fat man is Hans Von Hummel. The distinguished-looking one is F. James Kelly."

"You could be mistaken."

"Maybe . . . no, I'm positive. I saw Kelly once at the President's Inaugural Ball."

"Look around the room! Recognize anyone else?"

Tidi quickly did as she was told, scanning the main salon for a familiar face. "The old fellow with the funny-looking glasses sitting on the settee. That's Sir Eric Marks. The only other who looks vaguely familiar is the one who just came in, talking to Kirsti Fyrie. I'm pretty sure he's Jack Boyle, the Australian coal tycoon."

"How come you're such an authority on millionaires?"

Tidi gave a shrug. "You never know when you might meet one, so you prepare for the occasion even if it only comes off in your imagination."

"For once your daydreams paid off."

"I don't understand."

"Neither do I except this is beginning to look like a meeting of the clan."

Pitt began to get the uneasy feeling that coming into Rondheim's lair was a mistake. He was just in the process of thinking up an excuse to leave when Kirsti Fyrie spied them.

"Would you care to be seated in the study? We're almost ready to begin."

"Who is giving the reading?" Tidi asked.

Kirsti's face brightened. "Why, Oskar, of course."

Like a lamb to slaughter, he let Kirsti lead him to the study with Tidi tagging behind.

By the time they reached the study and found a

seat among the long circular rows of plush armchairs grouped around a raised dais, the room was nearly brimming to capacity. Kirsti Fyrie bowed her head toward the hushed bodies in the darkness and began to speak. "Ladies and gentlemen, distinguished guests. Tonight, our host, Mr. Oskar Rondheim, will offer for your enjoyment his latest work. This he will read in our native Icelandic tongue."

Five minutes after Rondheim began delivering his Icelandic saga in a rolling monotone, Pitt was sound asleep, content in the fact that no one would notice his lack of poetry appreciation in the darkened surroundings.

The audience's applause woke Pitt up. He stared at nothing in particular, stupidly gathering his thoughts. The lights had come on and he spent several moments blinking and getting his eyes accustomed to the glare. Rondheim was still on the dais, smugly accepting the generous acclaim. He held up his hands for silence.

"As most of you know, my favorite diversion is memorizing verse. With all due modesty, I must honestly state that my acquired knowledge is quite formidable. I would, at this time, like to put my reputation on the block and invite any of you in the audience to begin a line of any verse that comes to your mind. If I cannot finish the stanza that follows or complete the poem to your total satisfaction, I shall personally donate fifty thousand dollars to your favorite charity." He waited until the murmur of excited voices tapered to silence once more. "Shall we begin? Who will be first to challenge my memory?"

Rondheim looked about the room, a smile slowly spreading across his chiseled face as a familiar figure rose in the back. "Do you wish to try your luck, Major Pitt?"

Pitt looked at Rondheim somberly. "I can only offer you three words."

"I accept the challenge," Rondheim said confidently. "Please state them."

" 'God save thee,' " Pitt said very slowly, almost as if he were skeptical of any additional lines.

Rondheim laughed. "Elementary, Major. You've done me the kindness of allowing me to quote from my favorite verse." The contempt in Rondheim's voice was there; everyone in the room could feel it. " 'God save thee, ancient Mariner, From the fiends, that plague thee thus. Why look'st thou so? With my crossbow I shot the Albatross. The sun now rose upon the right. Out of the sea came he, Still hid in mist, and on the left Went down into the sea. And the good south wind still blew behind, But no sweet bird did follow, Nor any day for food or play Came to the mariners' hollo. And I had done a hellish thing, And it would work 'em woe. For all averr'd I had kill'd the bird That made the breeze to blow.' " Then suddenly Rondheim stopped, looking at Pitt curiously. "There's little need to continue. It's obvious to all present that you have asked me to quote 'The Rime of the Ancient Mariner' by Samuel Taylor Coleridge."

Pitt began to breathe a little easier. The light suddenly became brighter at the end of the tunnel. He knew something that he hadn't known before. It wasn't over yet, but things were looking up. The nightmare of Hunnewell's death would never trouble his sleep again.

A satisfied smile touched his lips. "Thank you, Mr. Rondheim. Your magnificent memory serves you well."

There was something about Pitt's tone that made Rondheim uneasy. "The pleasure is mine, Major." He didn't like the smile on Pitt's lips; he didn't like it at all.

Apart from himself, Oskar Rondheim, and Tidi, Pitt counted thirty-two men gathered around the flames crackling in the immense fireplace at the end of the trophy room. The reaction to Pitt's presence, as expressed by the faces, was interesting. No one even noticed him. For a fleeting moment he pictured himself a ghost with no substance that had just walked through the wall and was waiting for a séance to begin so that he could put in a spiritual appearance. Or so he thought. He could have imagined all sorts of strange scenes, but there was no imagining the blunt, circular gun barrel that was pressing into his spine.

He didn't bother to see whose hand held the gun. It would have made little difference. Rondheim answered any doubt.

A Russian, a short, stocky man with thinning hair, brown eyes and a limping gait, stood and faced Rondheim. "I believe you owe us an explanation, Mr. Rondheim. Why is this man," he nodded in Pitt's direction, "being treated like a criminal? You told myself and the other gentlemen here he is a newspaperman and that it would not be wise to speak too freely with him. Yet, that is the fourth or fifth time tonight you have referred to him as Major."

Rondheim studied the man before him, then set down his glass and pushed the button on a telephone. He didn't lift the receiver or talk into it, only picked up his glass and sipped at the remaining contents.

"Before your questions are answered, Comrade Tamareztov, I suggest you look behind you."

The Russian called Tamareztov swung around. Everyone swung around and looked to their rear. Not Pitt, he didn't have to. He kept his eyes straight ahead at a mirror that betrayed several hard-looking, expressionless men in black coveralls, who suddenly materialized at the opposite end of the room, AR-17 automatic rifles braced in the firing position.

A round-shouldered heavy character in his middle seventies, with blue knifing eyes deep set in a wizened face, grasped F. James Kelly by the arm. "You invited me to join you tonight, James. I think you know what this is all about."

"Yes, I do." When Kelly spoke, the pained look in his eyes was plainly visible. Then he turned away.

Slowly, very slowly, almost unnoticed, Kelly, Rondheim, Von Hummel, Marks and eight other men had grouped themselves on one side of the fireplace, leaving Pitt, Tidi, and the remaining guests standing opposite the flames in utter bewilderment. Pitt noted, with a touch of uneasiness, that all the guns were aimed at his group.

"I'm waiting, James," the old blue-eyed man said, his voice commanding.

Kelly hedged, looked rather sadly at Von Hummel and Marks. He waited expectantly. They finally nodded back, assuring him of their approval.

"Have any of you heard of Hermit Limited?"

The silence in the room became intense. Nobody spoke, nobody answered. Pitt was coolly calculating the chances of escape. He gave up, unable to bring the odds of success below fifty to one.

"Hermit Limited," Kelly went on, "is international in scope, but you won't find it on any stock exchange because it is vastly different in administration from any business you're familiar with. I don't have time to go into all the details of its operation, so just let me say that Hermit's main goal is to achieve control and take possession of South and of Central America."

"That's impossible," shouted a tall, raven-haired man with a pronounced French accent. "Absolutely unthinkable."

"It's also good business to do the impossible," Kelly said.

"What you've suggested is not business, but political power madness."

Kelly shook his head. "Madness maybe, but political power with selfish and inhuman motives, no." He searched the faces on the other side of the fireplace. They were all blank with disbelief.

"I am F. James Kelly," he said softly. "In my lifetime I have amassed over two billion dollars in assets.

"Two years ago I began thinking about what I would leave after I was gone. A financial empire fought over by parasitic business associates and relatives, who had only counted the days till my funeral so they could grab the spoils. Believe me, gentlemen, it was a pretty dismal thought. So I considered methods to distribute my assets in ways that would benefit mankind. But how? Andrew Carnegie built libraries, John D. Rockefeller set up foundations for science and education. What would do the most good for the peoples of the world regardless of white, black, yellow, red, or brown skins? Regardless of nationalities? If I had listened to my human emotions, it would have been an easy decision to use my money to assist the Cancer Crusade, the Red Cross, the Salvation Army or any one of the thousand medical centers or universities around the country. But was it really enough? Somehow it sounded too easy. I decided upon a different direction—one that would have a lasting impact on millions of people for hundreds of years."

"So you plotted to use your resources to become the self-proclaimed messiah of the poverty-stricken Latin nations," Pitt said.

Kelly offered Pitt a condescending smile. "No, you're quite mistaken, Major—ah—"

"Pitt," Rondheim provided. "Major Dirk Pitt."

Kelly gazed at Pitt thoughtfully. "Are you by chance any relation to Senator George Pitt?"

"His son," Pitt acknowledged.

Kelly stood like a wax statue for a moment. He

turned to Rondheim but only received a stone face in return. "Your father is a good friend," he said woodenly.

"*Was,*" Pitt said coldly.

Kelly fought to keep his composure. It was apparent that the man was deeply troubled by his conscience. "Whatever path I chose had to come from a means far more calculating, far less emotional than the human mind."

"Computers!" the word fell from the lips of Kelly's elderly friend. "Hermit Limited was the project you programmed into the computers at our data processing division nearly two years ago. I remember it well, James. You closed down the entire complex for three months. Gave everyone a vacation with pay—a display of generosity that you've seldom demonstrated before or since. Loaned the use of the equipment, you said, to the government for a top secret military project."

"I was afraid even then you might have guessed my intentions, Sam." It was the first time Kelly had called the old gentleman by name. "But systems analysis provided the only efficient solution to the problem I presented myself. The concept could hardly be classed as revolutionary. Every government has its think tanks. The space systems devised for our rocketry and moon projects have been utilized for everything from diagnosing crime reports to improving surgical procedures. Programming a computer to select a country or geographic location that is ripe for a controlled and developed utopian atmosphere and the method to achieve that goal is not as farfetched as any of you might think."

"The American government will take a very dim view to your grandiose scheme," said a tall man with white hair, white eyebrows and solemn eyes.

"By the time their agents have penetrated Hermit Limited's organization we will have proven our intentions with solid accomplishments," Kelly said. "They will not bother us. In fact, I predict they will discreetly give us a green light and provide whatever aid they consider possible without international repercussion."

"I take it you don't intend to go it alone," Pitt probed.

"No," Kelly tersely answered. "After I satisfied myself that the program was sound and had every chance to succeed, I approached Marks, Von Hummel, Boyle and the other gentlemen you see here who possessed the financial means to make it a reality. They thought as I did. Money is to be used for the common good of all. Why die and leave nothing but a large bank account or a few corporations that soon forget who planted their seed and nourished them to financial maturity? We then met and formed Hermit Limited. Each of us owns equal shares of stock and has an equal voice on the board of directors."

"How do you know one or more of your partners in crime won't get greedy?" Pitt smiled faintly. "They may swindle a country or two for themselves."

"The computer chose well," Kelly said, undaunted. "Look at us. No one is under the age of sixty-five. What do we have left? One, two, maybe with luck ten years. We are all childless. Therefore, no heirs. What does any one of us have to gain by excessive avarice? The answer is simple. Nothing."

The Russian shook his head incredulously. "Your scheme is absurd. Even my own government would never consider such drastic and reckless action."

"Your grand design has a flaw," Pitt said. "A deviation that could easily screw up the works."

Kelly stared at Pitt speculatively. "Your brain against the most advanced techniques of computer science? Come now, Major. We've spent months programming every possibility, every abnormality. You're merely playing games."

"Am I? How do you explain Rondheim and Miss Fyrie? They hardly pass the age requirements for executive material of Hermit Limited. Rondheim is short by twenty years. Miss Fyrie . . . well, ah . . . she doesn't even come close."

"Miss Fyrie's brother, Kristjan, was an idealist, like myself, a man who was searching for a way to raise people from the mud of poverty and misery. His acts of generosity in Africa and other parts of the world where his business transpired led us to make an exception. Unlike most hardheaded businessmen, he used his wealth for common good. When he tragically lost his life, we, the board of directors of Hermit Limited," he bowed to the men seated around him, "voted to elect Miss Fyrie in his place."

"And Rondheim?"

"A fortunate contingency we had hoped for, but not counted on. Though his extensive fishing facilities appeared an enticing asset toward developing the fishing industry of South America, it was his hidden talents and useful connections that swung the pendulum in his favor."

"The superintendent of your assassination department?" Pitt said grimly.

The men around Kelly looked at each other, then at Pitt. They looked in silence with curiosity written on their faces. Von Hummel wiped his brow for the fiftieth time and Sir Eric Marks rubbed his hand across his lips and nodded at Kelly, a movement that did not go unnoticed by Pitt.

"You guessed that?" Kelly said in an even voice.

"Hardly," Pitt said. "After you've had three attempts on your life, you kind of get to know these things."

"The hydroplane!" Rondheim snapped savagely. "You know what happened to it?"

"Terribly sloppy of you, my dear Oskar, or should I say the late captain of your last boat. You should have seen the look on his face just before my Molotov cocktail hit him. One thing is certain. Due to your negligence, you'll never see your hydroplane and crew again."

"Can't you see what he's trying to do?" Rondheim took a step toward Pitt. "He's trying to turn us against each other."

"That will do!" Kelly's tone was cold, his eyes commanding. "Please go on, Major."

"You're very kind. Poor Oskar also bumbled the second attempt. I don't have to go into the sorry details, but I'm sure you're aware that his two feeble-brained assassins are talking on a party line right this minute to agents of the National Intelligence Agency."

Kelly spun around to Rondheim. "Is that true?"

"My men never talk." Rondheim glared at Pitt. "They know what will happen to their relatives if they do. Besides, they know nothing."

"Let us hope you're right," Kelly said heavily. He came and stood over Pitt, staring with a strangely expressionless gaze that was more disturbing than any display of animosity could ever have been. "This game has gone far enough, Major."

"Too bad. I was just getting warmed up, just getting to the good part."

"It isn't necessary."

"Neither was killing Dr. Hunnewell," Pitt said. His voice was unnaturally calm. "A terrible, terrible mistake, a sad miscalculation. Doubly so, since the good doctor was a key member of Hermit Limited."

10

Kelly's eyes widened and his breath seemed to stop. Then slowly he began to gain control again, calm, quiet, the professional businessman, saying nothing until the right words formed in his mind.

"Your computers must have blown a fuse," Pitt continued. "Admiral Sandecker and I were on to Dr. Hunnewell right from the start." Pitt lied, knowing there was no way Kelly or Rondheim could prove otherwise. "You wouldn't be interested in how or why."

"You are mistaken, Major," Kelly said impatiently. "We would be most interested."

Pitt took a deep breath and made the plunge. "Actually our first tipoff came when Dr. Len Matajic was rescued—"

"No! That cannot be," Rondheim gasped.

Pitt gave silent thanks to Sandecker for his wild plan to resurrect the ghosts of Matajic and O'Riley. "Pick up the phone and ask the overseas operator for Room 409 at Walter Reed General Hospital in Washington. I suggest you request person-to-person; your call will go through faster."

"That will not be necessary," Kelly said. "I have no reason to doubt you."

"Suit yourself," Pitt said carelessly, fighting to keep a straight face, laying his bluff successfully. "As I started to say, when Dr. Matajic was rescued, he described the *Lax* and its crew in vivid detail. He wasn't fooled for a minute by the alterations to the superstructure. But, of course, you know all this. Your people monitored his message to Admiral Sandecker."

"And then?"

"Don't you see? The rest was simple deduction. Thanks to Matajic's description, it didn't take any great effort to trace the ship's whereabouts from the time it disappeared with Kristjan Fyrie to when it moored on the iceberg where Matajic had his research station." Pitt smiled. "Because of Dr. Matajic's powers of observation—the crew's suntans hardly spelled a fishing trip in North Atlantic waters—Admiral Sandecker was able to figure the *Lax*'s previous course along the South American coast. He then began to suspect Dr. Hunnewell. Rather clever of the admiral now that I look back on it."

"Go on, go on," Kelly urged.

"Well, obviously the *Lax* had been utilizing the undersea probe to find new mineral deposits. And just as obviously, with Fyrie and his engineers dead, Dr. Hunnewell, the co-inventor of the probe, was the only one around who knew how to operate it."

"You are exceedingly well informed," Kelly said wryly. "But that hardly constitutes proof."

Pitt was on tricky ground. So far he had been able to skirt around the National Intelligence Agency's involvement in Hermit Limited. And Kelly had yet to be baited into offering any further information. It's time, he amusedly told himself, to tell the truth.

"Proof is it? Okay, will you accept the words of a dying man? Straight from the horse's mouth. The man in question is Dr. Hunnewell himself."

"I don't believe it."

"His last words before he died in my arms were: 'God save thee.' "

"What are you talking about?" Rondheim shouted. "What are you trying to do?"

"I meant to thank you for that, Oskar," Pitt said coldly. "Hunnewell knew who his murderer was— the man who gave the order for his death. He tried to quote from 'The Rime of the Ancient Mariner.' It was all there, wasn't it? You quoted it yourself: 'Why look'st thou so? With my crossbow I shot the Albatross.' Your trademark, Oskar, the red albatross. That's what Hunnewell meant. 'For all averr'd I had kill'd the bird That made the breeze to blow.' You killed the man who helped you probe the sea floor."

"You sent your arrow in the right direction, Major Pitt." Kelly idly stared at the smoke from his cigar. "But you aimed at the wrong man. I gave the order for Dr. Hunnewell's death. Oskar merely carried it through."

"For what purpose?"

"Dr. Hunnewell was beginning to have second thoughts about Hermit Limited's methods of operation—quite old-fashioned thoughts really: thou shall not kill and all that. He threatened to expose our entire organization unless we closed down our assassination department. A condition that was impossible to accept if we were to have any chance for ultimate success. Therefore, Dr. Hunnewell had to be discharged from the firm."

"Another business principle, of course."

Kelly smiled. "It is that."

"And I had to be swept under the carpet because I was a witness," Pitt said as if answering a question.

Kelly simply nodded.

"But the undersea probe?" Pitt asked. "With Hunnewell and Fyrie—the geese who laid the golden eggs—dead, who is left with the knowledge to build a second-generation model?"

The confident look was back in Kelly's eyes. "No one," he answered softly. "But then no one is required. You see, our computers have now been programmed with the necessary information. With proper analysis of the data, we should have a working model of the probe within ninety days."

For a brief moment, Pitt stood silent, caught unprepared by the unexpected disclosure. Then he quickly shook off his surprise at Kelly's statement.

"Then Hunnewell no longer served a useful purpose. Your data-processing brains discovered the secret of producing celtinium-279."

"I compliment you, Major Pitt. You possess a penetrating discernment." Kelly glanced impatiently at his watch and nodded to Rondheim. Then he turned and said, "I'm sorry, but I'm afraid the time has come, gentlemen. The party is over."

"What do you intend on doing with us, James?" Sam's eyes burned into Kelly's until the billionaire turned and avoided the stare. "It's obvious you told us your secrets as a courtesy to our curiosity. It's also obvious you can never let us walk from this house with those secrets in our heads."

"It's true." Kelly looked at the men standing opposite the fireplace. "None of you can be permitted to tell what you heard here tonight."

"But why?" old Sam asked philosophically. "Why expose us to your clandestine operation and thereby seal our death warrants?"

Kelly tiredly rubbed his eyes and leaned back in a large overstuffed leather chair. "The moment of truth, the denouement." He sadly searched the faces across the room. They were pale with shock and disbelief.

"It is now eleven o'clock. In exactly forty-two hours and ten minutes, Hermit Limited will open its doors for business. Twenty-four hours later we will be running the affairs of our first client, or country, if you prefer. In order to make this historical event as inauspicious as possible, we need a diversion. A disaster that will attract headlines and cause anxious concern among the leaders of world governments while our plan is carried off practically unnoticed."

"And we are your diversion," said the tall white-haired man with the solemn eyes.

After a long wordless stare, Kelly simply said, "Yes."

"This must be some sort of insane joke," Tamareztov shouted. "You cannot simply shoot two dozen men and their wives down like animals."

"Your wives will be returned to your lodgings safe and unharmed, and unknowing." Kelly set his glass on the mantel. "We have no intention of shooting anyone. We intend to rely on Mother Nature to do the job, with a little help, of course. After all, shootings can be traced, accidents merely regretted."

Rondheim motioned the black coveralled men with the guns to move in closer. "If you please, gentlemen, roll up one of your sleeves."

As if on cue, Kirsti left the room and quickly returned carrying a small tray set with bottles and hypodermic syringes. She set the tray down and began filling the syringes.

Rondheim turned to Pitt. "Come into the next room, Major. In your instance, I shall deal with you on a personal basis." He waved the gun he had taken from Kirsti toward a doorway.

Rondheim, followed by two of his guards, escorted Pitt along a wide hall, down a circular flight of stairs into another hall, then shoved him roughly through the second of several doorways lining both sides of the second passageway. Pitt, letting himself go loose, stumbled awkwardly, fell to the floor, then scanned the room.

It was an immense room, painted stark white; a large pad lay in the middle of the floor, surrounded by an array of body-building equipment, brightly lit by long rows of fluorescent light fixtures. The room was a gymnasium, better and more expensively equipped than any Pitt had ever seen. The walls were decorated with at least fifty posters depicting the many karate movements. Pitt silently acknowledged a well-conceived and laid-out training room.

"Tell me, Major. Are you familiar with karate or Kung-Fu?"

As if to answer, Pitt threw back his head and spun sideways in one convulsive movement. He had caught the beginning of the lightning thrust as the Icelander came in with a reverse punch that connected on Pitt's cheekbone, a half-solid blow that would have caused much more damage than a bruised swelling if Pitt hadn't rolled with the impact.

Pitt had made a mistake by ducking, had almost given himself away by revealing his quick reflexes. He had to fight to keep his mind turned on the rules. It wasn't easy. He gritted his teeth and waited.

Rondheim scored with a roundhouse kick to the head, knocking him off the mat against a row of horizontal exercise bars set into the wall. Pitt lay on the floor in silence, tasting the blood from his crushed lips and feeling his loosened teeth.

Rondheim lost no time in working on him again. A quick combination of sledgehammer blows to the head that never seemed to end, followed by a front kick to the exposed rib area, and Pitt felt rather than heard one of his ribs snap. As if in slow motion, Pitt sunk to his knees and slowly slumped forward onto his face.

The daggerlike pain in his chest and the agony of his torn face rose in giant waves and pounded him to the verge of blackness; yet he was surprised to find his mind was still functioning normally. Instead of allowing the painless oblivion of unconsciousness to swoop in, he willed himself to fake it, setting his teeth against a groan.

Rondheim was infuriated. "I'm not through with you yet." He motioned to one of the guards. "Revive him."

Pitt coughed once, twice, then spit a gob of blood on the guard's boot, taking grim satisfaction that it was no accident. He rolled over onto his side and looked up at Rondheim looming over him.

Rondheim laughed softly. "You seem to have difficulty staying awake in class, Major. Perhaps you are becoming bored." His voice suddenly chilled. "Stand up! You have yet to finish your—ah—course of instruction."

And then Rondheim leaned down and struck Pitt with a shuto blow to the back of the neck. There was no fighting it, no faking it this time: Pitt blacked out for real.

Rondheim turned to the guards. "Throw him in with the others," he ordered. "If he is fortunate and opens his eyes once more, he can have the satisfaction of knowing he died among friends."

11

Somewhere in the black pit of unconsciousness Pitt began to see light. It was vague, dim like the bulb of a flashlight whose batteries were gasping out their last breath of energy. He struggled toward it and focused his eyes with difficulty. Tidi was gazing down at him. Then a voice spoke.

"Did you get the license number of the truck, Major? Or was it a bulldozer that mashed your already ugly profile?"

Pitt turned his head and looked into the smiling, but tight-muscled face of Jerome P. Lillie. "Would you believe a giant with muscles like tree trunks?"

Pitt pulled himself to a sitting position and gazed in agony through a red haze of pain as his broken rib cried in protest. The unthinking sudden movement made his side feel as if someone had squeezed his chest between a giant pair of pliers and twisted. Carefully, gently, he eased himself forward until he could see around him.

The sight that met his eyes looked like something

out of a nightmare. For a long moment he stared at the unreal scene and then at Tidi and Lillie, his face a study of bewildered incomprehension. Then a shred of understanding crept into his head and with it some certainty of where he was. He reached out a hand to steady himself and muttered to no one in particular.

"It's not possible."

For maybe ten seconds, maybe twenty, Pitt sat there, stiff and unmoving, staring at the broken helicopter a scant ten yards away. The jagged remains of the hulk lay half sunk in mud at the bottom of a deep ravine whose walls rose in sharp sloping angles to seemingly come together and meet a hundred feet toward the Iceland sky. He noted that the shattered craft was large, probably one of the Titan class, capable of carrying thirty passengers. Whatever colors or markings the copter may have been painted originally, it was impossible to recognize them now. Most of the fuselage back of the cockpit was crumpled like a bellows, the remaining framework a myriad of twisted metal.

Pitt's first impression, the one that ruled his confused mind, was that no one from the crash could have lived. But there they were: Pitt, Tidi, Lillie, and scattered about the steep slopes of the ravine in unnatural pain-contorted positions, the same group of men who had stood beside Pitt in Rondheim's trophy room, the same group who had opposed F. James Kelly and Hermit Limited.

They all appeared to be alive, but most were badly

injured; the grotesque angles of their arms and legs revealed a terrible array of smashed and broken bones.

"Sorry to ask the inescapable question," Pitt mumbled, his voice hoarse, though now under control, "but . . . what happened?"

"Not what you think," Lillie replied.

"What then? It's obvious . . . Rondheim was abducting all of us somewhere when the aircraft crashed."

"We didn't crash," Lillie said. "The wreck has been here for days, maybe even weeks."

Pitt stared incredulously at Lillie, who seemed to be lying comfortably on the damp ground, oblivious of the wetness soaking through his clothing. "You'd better fill me in. What happened to these people? How did you come to be here? Everything."

"Not too much to my story," Lillie said quietly. "Rondheim's men caught me snooping around the Albatross docks. Before I had a chance to uncover anything, they hustled me off to Rondheim's house and threw me in with these other gentlemen."

Pitt made a move toward Lillie. "You're in pretty rough shape. Let's have a look."

Impatiently Lillie waved him back.

"Hear me out. Then get away from here and get help. No one is in immediate danger of dying from their injuries—Rondheim saw to that. Our primary peril is exposure. The temperature is under forty degrees now. In another few hours it will be freezing. After that, the cold and the shock will take the first

of us. By morning there will be nothing in this
ravine but frozen bodies."

"Rondheim saw to that? I'm afraid—"

"You don't get it? You're slow on the trigger,
Major Pitt. It's obvious, the carnage you see here
was never caused by accident. Immediately after
our sadistic friend Rondheim beat you to a pulp, we
were each given a heavy dose of Nembutal and
then, very coldly and methodically, he and his men
took us one at a time and fractured whatever bones
they thought were necessary to make it appear as
though we were all injured in the crash of the helicopter."

Pitt stared at Lillie but said nothing. Totally off
balance, his mind was in a whirlpool of disbelief, his
thought desperately seeking to sort out a set of circumstances that defied comprehension. The way he
felt, he would have been prepared to believe anything, but Lillie's words were too macabre, too mon-
strous to consider.

"But for what purpose? Why the savagery? Kelly
could have simply put us on another aircraft and
dropped it over the ocean without a trace, with no
chance for survivors."

"Computers are a hard lot; they only deal in cold
facts," Lillie murmured wearily. "To their respective
governments, the men suffering around us are important figures. You were at Rondheim's little party.
You heard Kelly explain why they had to die—their
deaths are meant to be a diversion, to buy time and
to grab headlines and the attention of world leaders

while Hermit Limited pulls off its coup without international interference."

"What's to stop someone from accidentally discovering us at any moment?" Tidi asked.

"It's fairly obvious," Pitt said, thoughtfully surveying the immediate surroundings. "We can't be seen unless that someone is standing practically on top of us. Add to that the fact we're probably in the most uninhabited area of Iceland, and the odds of being found begin to stretch to infinity."

"Now you can clearly see the picture," Lillie said. "The helicopter had to be placed in the narrow confines of the ravine and then destroyed because it could not have been purposely crashed with any degree of accuracy—a perfect undetectable location. A search plane directly overhead could have no more than a second to spot the debris, a million-to-one chance at best. The next step was to scatter our bodies around the area. Then, after two or three weeks, the most a competent coroner could determine is that some of us died from injuries sustained from the phony crash and the rest from exposure and shock."

"Am I the only one who can walk?" Pitt asked harshly. His broken ribs ached like a thousand sores, but the hopeful stares, the miserable bit of optimism in the eyes of the men who knew death was only a few hours away, forced him to ignore the pain.

"A few can walk," Lillie answered. "But with broken arms, they'll never make it to the top of the ravine."

"Then I guess I'm elected."

"You're elected." Lillie smiled faintly. "If it's any consolation, you have the satisfaction of knowing Rondheim is up against a tougher man than his computers projected."

The encouragement in Lillie's eyes became the extra impetus Pitt needed. He rose unsteadily to his feet and looked down at the figure lying stiffly on the ground.

"Where did Rondheim bust you?"

"Both shoulders and—I'm guessing—my pelvis." Lillie's tone was as calm as if he were describing the fractured surface of the moon.

"Ouch." Pitt turned away and knelt over Tidi.

"Where did they hurt you?"

"My ankles are a little off center." She smiled gamely. "Nothing serious. I'm just lucky, I guess."

"I'm sorry," Pitt said. "You wouldn't be lying here if it wasn't for my bungling."

She took his hand and squeezed it. "It's more exciting than taking dictation and typing the admiral's letters."

Pitt stumbled awkwardly once more to his feet and walked unsteadily over the water-soaked ground to the old man he knew simply as Sam. He thought of the distinguished manner, the warm, piercing eyes he had seen in the trophy room as he stared down and saw the legs, twisted outwards like the crooked branches of an oak tree, the blue eyes dulled by pain, and he forced himself to smile a confident, hopeful smile.

"Hang in there, Sam." Pitt leaned over and shook

Sam's hand. The blue eyes suddenly came to life and the old man raised up, gripping Pitt's outstretched hand with an intensity that Pitt didn't think was possible, and the lines of the tired, drawn face lightened into determined hardness.

"He must be stopped, Major Pitt." The voice was low, almost an insistent whisper. "James must not be allowed to go through with this terrible thing. His purpose glories in goodness, but the people he has surrounded himself with, glory only in greed and power."

Pitt only nodded without speaking.

"I forgive James for what he has done." Sam was talking, almost rambling to himself. "Tell him his brother forgives—"

"I can't believe it!" Pitt's shock showed in his face. "You're brothers?"

"Yes, James is my younger brother. I remained in the background these many years, handling the financial details and problems that plague a giant multinational corporation. James, a master at wheeling and dealing, enjoyed the center of attraction. Until now, we were a pretty successful combination." Sam Kelly bowed his head in a barely perceptible sign of farewell. "I wish you luck."

"Thanks," Pitt murmured. He turned away and began climbing the embankment toward the top of the ravine.

Cautiously at first, a few inches at a time, trying to move at a pace that favored his cracked ribs, Pitt clawed at the soft, slippery earth and pulled himself upward without looking in any direction except straight ahead. The first twenty feet were easy. Then the slope steepened and the soil became more firm, making it difficult to dig the shallow hand and toe-holds which afforded his only source of support.

The climb itself was sheer torture, punctuated by the agony of his injuries. All emotion had drained away, his movements became mechanical, dig and pull, dig and pull. He tried to keep count of each foot gained but lost track after thirty, his mind totally void of all mental function.

He began counting again, only this time he stopped at ten. Then one minute of rest, he told himself, no more, and he began again. His breath was coming in heaving gulps now, his fingers were raw, the ends of the nails jagged and spotted with blood, his arm muscles aching from the continuous effort— a sure sign his body was about spent. Sweat trickled down his face, but the irritating tickle could not be felt through his agonized flesh. He paused and looked up, seeing little through the swollen slits that were his eyes. The edge of the ravine blended into a nebulous line of angles and shadowy profiles that defied any judgment of distance.

And then suddenly, almost with a sense of surprise, Pitt's hands found the soft, crumbling edge of the slope. With strength he didn't think was possible, he pulled himself up onto flat ground and rolled over on his back, lying inert and, to all appearances, dead.

For nearly five minutes, Pitt lay rigid, only his chest moving with the pulsating rise and fall of his breath. Slowly, as the waves of total exhaustion receded to a level of sufferable tolerance, he pulled himself to his feet and peered into the bottom of the narrow chasm at the tiny figures below. He cupped his hands to yell, then decided against it. There were no words he could think of to shout that had any meaning, any encouragement. All the people below could see was his head and shoulders over the level of the steep cliff. Then with a wave of the hand, he was gone.

12

Pitt stood like a solitary tree on a great empty plain. A dark green mosslike vegetation spread in every direction as far as he could see, edged on one horizon by a range of high hills and cloaked by a sun-whitened mist on two others. Except for a few small rises dotting the desolate landscape, most of the ground was nearly flat. At first he thought he was completely alone. But then he saw a tiny snipe that soared across the sky like a dart in search of an unseen target. It came closer, and from a height of two hundred feet it circled and looked down at Pitt, as if curiously inspecting the strange animal that stood out so vividly in red and yellow plumage against the center of the unending green carpet. After three cursory sweeps, the little bird's inquisitiveness waned and it fluttered its wings against the air and continued on its seeming flight to nowhere.

It didn't take any great ingenious deduction to determine that he was somewhere in the middle of the uninhabited part of Iceland. The island stretched one hundred ninety miles from north to south, he recalled, and nearly three hundred miles from east to west. Since the shortest distance between two points was north and south, the other two directions were eliminated. If he traveled south, there was every possibility that he would run onto the Vatnajökull ice mass, not only Iceland's but Europe's largest glacier, a great frozen wall that would have signaled the end of everything.

North it was, he decided. The logic behind his decision bordered on the primitive, but there was another reason, a compelling urge to outsmart the computers by traveling in the direction least expected, a direction that offered the least obvious chance of success. The average man in similar circumstances would have probably headed toward Reykjavik, the largest sprawl of civilization, far to the west and south. That is undoubtedly, he hoped, what the computers had been programmed for—the average man.

A light suddenly clicked on deep in the recesses of his brain. A long-forgotten bit of outdoor lore he'd learned many years before during a four-day hike in the Sierras with his old Boy Scout troop began to break through the fog-shrouded barrier of time.

It took him nearly ten minutes of searching before he found a small pool of water trapped in a shallow depression beneath a dome-shaped hill. Quickly, as dexterously as his raw and bleeding fingers would allow, Pitt unclasped his tie and tore off the pin that held it in place. Wrapping one end of the long silk material around his knee, he knelt and pulled it taut with his left hand and with his right began stroking the pin from head to tip in a single direction against the silk, building friction and magnetizing the tiny piece of metal.

When he felt satisfied that further friction would add nothing more, he rubbed the pin over his forehead and nose, covering it with as much skin oil as it could hold. Then he took two slender bits of thread from the lining of his jacket and doubled them loosely around the pin.

Feeling he was ready, he gingerly picked up the two loops and with painstaking slowness lowered the pin into the calm little pond. Holding a deep breath, Pitt watched the water bend under the weight of the metal. Then ever so gently his fingers cautiously slid the threads apart until the pin swam by itself, kept afloat by the oil and the surface tension of the water.

Only a child at Christmastime, staring wide-eyed at an array of gifts under the tree, could have experienced the same feeling of wonder that Pitt did that moment as he sat entranced and watched that crazy little pin swing leisurely in a half circle until its head pointed toward magnetic north. He sat there unmoving for a full three minutes, staring at his makeshift compass, almost afraid that if he blinked his eyes, it would sink and disappear.

"Let's see your computer come up with that one," Pitt murmured to the empty air.

A tenderfoot might have impatiently started running in the direction the pin pointed, mistaken in the assumption that a compass always faithfully aims its point toward true north. Pitt knew that the only place where a compass would unerringly indicate the North Pole was a small area in the Great Lakes between the United States and Canada where by chance the North and Magnetic Poles come into line. As an experienced navigator, he was also aware that the Magnetic Pole lay somewhere beneath Prince of Wales Island above Hudson Bay, approximately one thousand miles below the Arctic Pole and only a few hundred miles above Iceland. That meant that the pin was pointing a few degrees north of west. Pitt figured his compass declination at about eighty degrees, a rough guess at best, but at least he was certain that north now stood at a near right angle to the head of the pin.

Pitt took his bearing and picked the rudimentary compass needle out of the water and started walking into the mist. Luck was with him and the mist disappeared after an hour and a half, offering him a chance to take advantage of the many hot springs he passed and orient his bearings with the compass pin. Now he could line up a landmark to the north and keep shifting from one landmark to the next until he was sure he was straying. Then he would stop and take another compass reading and begin the process over again.

Two hours became three. Three hours became four. Each minute was an infinite unit of misery and suffering, of aching cold, of intense burning pain, of fighting for control of his mind. Time melted into an eternity which Pitt knew might not end until he fell against the soft, damp grass for the last time. In spite of his determination, he began to have doubts that he would live through the next few hours.

One step in front of the other, an endless cycle that slowly pushed Pitt further and further into total exhaustion. His thoughts had no room now for anything but the next landmark, and when he reached it, he concentrated every ounce of his sinking energy on the next one. Logic was nearly nonexistent. Only when he heard a muted alarm going off somewhere in the dim corners of his brain, warning him that he was straying off course, did he stop at a steaming sulfur pool to regain a heading with his compass.

His puffed eyes were almost totally closed, his legs cramped from exhaustion, and his breath coming in agonized gasps that broke the clear still air, but he struggled to his feet and stumbled forward, urged on by an inner strength he didn't know existed. For the next two hours he blundered along in a void all of his own. Then, in the middle of climbing a small eight-foot embankment, his body turned off the switch to consciousness and collapsed like a deflated balloon just inches from the top of the ridge.

Pitt knew he had crossed over the threshold from physical sensibility to the inertness of twilight sleep. But something didn't quite jell. His body was dead; all pain was gone, all feeling, even human emotion seemingly had died. Yet, he could still see, though his total panorama consisted only of grass-covered ground no more than a few inches in front of his eyes. And he could hear, his ears relayed a throbbing sound to a numbed brain that refused to relay any explanation as to the cause or the distance from which the strange coughing beat came.

A pair of boots, two worn leather boots, stood in front of Pitt's unseeing eyes where only a moment before was an empty plot of wild grass. And then phantom hands rolled him over on his back and he became aware of a face framed by the vacant sky—a stern face with sea-blue eyes. Gray hair flowed around a broad forehead like the helmet on a warrior in a Flemish painting. An old man, aged somewhere beyond seventy years, wearing a worn turtleneck sweater, bent and touched Pitt's face.

Then without saying a word, with surprising strength for a man of his years, he lifted Pitt up and carried him over the rise. Through the cobwebs of his mind, Pitt began to wonder at the sheer coincidence, the miracle, which indeed it was, that led to his discovery. No more than one easy stride over the small summit lay a road; he had fallen within spitting distance of a small dirt road that paralleled a tumbling glacial river of white froth, rushing swiftly through a narrow gorge of black lava rock. Yet the sound Pitt's ears had detected came not from the roar of the falling water, but from the exhaust of an engine belonging to a battered, dust-covered British-made jeep.

Like a child placing a doll in a highchair, the old Icelander set Pitt in the front passenger seat of the jeep. Then he climbed behind the wheel and steered the rugged little vehicle over the winding road. They stopped in front of a small farmhouse with white sideboards and a red roof. Pitt shrugged off the supporting hands and staggered into the living room of the comfortable little house.

"A telephone, quickly. I need a telephone."

The blue eyes narrowed. "You are English?" the Icelander asked slowly in a heavy Nordic accent.

"American," Pitt answered impatiently. "There are two dozen seriously injured people out there who will die if we don't get help to them soon."

"There are others on the plateau?" There was no concealing the astonishment.

"Yes, yes!" Pitt nodded his head violently.

The Icelander shrugged helplessly. "The nearest telephone lines are forty kilometers away."

A great tidal wave of despair swept over Pitt only to ebb and vanish at the stranger's next words.

"However, I have a radio transmitter." He motioned to a side room. "Please, this way."

Pitt followed him into a small, well-lit, but spartan room, the three primary pieces of furniture being a chair, a cabinet and an ancient hand-carved table holding a gleaming transmitter, not more than a few months from manufacture; Pitt could only marvel at the latest equipment being used in an isolated farmhouse. The Icelander crossed hurriedly to the transmitter, sat down and began twisting the array of dials and knobs. He switched the radio to SEND, selected the frequency and picked up the microphone.

He spoke a few words rapidly in Icelandic and waited. Nothing came back over the speaker. He shifted the transmitting frequency fractionally and spoke again. This time a voice answered almost immediately. After ten minutes of explanation and translation, Pitt requested and received a call from the American Embassy.

"Where in the world have you been?" Sandecker's voice exploded over the speaker so loudly that it might have come from the doorway.

"Waiting for a streetcar, walking in the park," Pitt snapped back. "It makes no difference. How soon before a team of medics can be assembled and in the air?"

There was a tense silence before the admiral answered. There was, he knew, a tone of urgent insistence in Pitt's voice, a tone Sandecker had seldom heard from Pitt's lips. "I can have a team of Air Force paramedics ready to load in thirty minutes," he said slowly. "Would you mind telling me the reason behind your request for a medical unit?"

Pitt didn't answer immediately. His thoughts were barely able to focus. He nodded thankfully as the Icelander offered him the chair.

"Every minute we waste with explanations, someone may die. Admiral," Pitt implored, "contact the Air Force and get their paramedics loaded on helicopters and supplied to aid victims of an air disaster. Then while there's time, I can fill you in on the details."

"Understood," Sandecker said without wasting a word. "Stand by."

Pitt nodded again, this time to himself, and slumped dejectedly in the chair. It won't be long now, he thought, if only they're in time. He felt a hand on his shoulder, half turned and managed a crooked smile up at the warm-eyed Icelander.

"I've been a rude guest," he said quietly. "I haven't introduced myself or thanked you for saving my life."

The old man offered a long, weathered hand. "Golfur Andursson," he said. "I am chief gillie for the Rarfur River."

Pitt gripped Andursson's hand and introduced himself and then asked, "A chief gillie?"

"Yes, a gillie is also the river warden. We act as guides for fishermen and watch over the ecology of the river, much like a conservationist in your own country who protects the natural resources of your inland water grounds."

"It must be lonely work—" Pitt's mouth stopped working and he gasped as a sharp pain in his chest nearly carried him into blackness. He clutched the table, fighting to remain conscious.

"Come," Andursson said. "You must let me tend to your injuries."

"No," Pitt answered firmly. "I must stay by the radio. I'm not leaving this chair."

Andursson hesitated. Then he shook his head and said nothing. He disappeared from the room and returned in less than two minutes carrying a large first-aid case. He had just finished binding Pitt's chest when the radio crackled and Sandecker's gravel voice broke into the room again.

"Major Pitt, do you read me?"

Pitt lifted the microphone and pressed the transmitting switch. "Pitt here. I read you, Admiral."

"The paramedics are mustering at Keflavik and Iceland's civilian search and rescue units are standing by. I'll maintain radio contact and coordinate their efforts." There was a momentary silence. "You have a lot of worried people here. Keflavik has no report of a missing plane, either military or commercial."

Rondheim wasn't taking any chances, Pitt thought. He was taking his own sweet time about reporting his overdue and missing guests.

"Notification isn't scheduled yet."

Total uncomprehension broke in Sandecker's voice. "Come again. Please repeat."

"Trust me, Admiral. I can't even begin to answer a tenth of the questions that must be running through everyone's mind, especially over the radio—I repeat—especially over the radio."

Pitt flicked off the mike switch and turned to Andursson. "How far is the nearest town and in what direction?"

Andursson vaguely pointed out the window. "Sodafoss . . . we are exactly fifty kilometers south of its town square."

Pitt quickly added to the Icelander's figure to allow for the distance he had stumbled across the plateau and turned back to the radio. "The aircraft came down approximately eighty kilometers north of Sodafoss. I repeat, eighty kilometers north of Sodafoss."

Outside, unnoticed by Pitt, the sun, a perfect orange disk in the northern latitudes, was being rapidly overtaken by great rolling black clouds that soon surrounded and cut off its bright glow. A chilling breeze had sprung up and was bending the grass in the meadows and hills. Pitt became aware of Andursson's hand on his shoulder and the sudden dimming light in the room at the same time.

"A storm from the north," Andursson said solemnly. "It will snow within the hour."

Pitt threw back the chair and hurriedly crossed the room to a small double window. He stared through the glass, his eyes unbelieving, and he struck his fist against the wall in despair. Then he turned to Andursson.

"I need to use the radio again, and I need some blades."

The old man looked more lost than ever. "Blades?"

"Yes, propeller blades. Three of them, to be exact."

13

There are many wondrous sights to behold in this world, but to Pitt nothing, not even a thirty-story rocket blasting into outer space or a needle-nosed supersonic transport streaking across the sky at twice the speed of sound could ever look half as incredibly beautiful as that old Ford tri-motor, the famed Tin Goose, pitching and rolling awkwardly in the fitful wind, curtained by the black folds of giant menacing clouds. Braced against the increasing gale, he watched intently as the ancient aircraft, graceful in its ugliness, circled Andursson's farm once before the pilot eased back on the throttles, skimmed less than ten feet over a fence and set it down in the meadow where the wide-set landing wheels rolled to a complete stop in less than two hundred feet from touchdown.

Pitt turned to Andursson. "Well, good-by, Golfur. Thank you for all you've done for me . . . for all of us."

Golfur Andursson shook Pitt's hand. "It is I who

thank you, Major. For the honor and opportunity to help my fellow brother."

Pitt couldn't run, his cracked ribs wouldn't permit that, but he covered the distance to the tri-motor in less than thirty seconds. Just as he reached the right side of the fuselage, the door flew open and willing arms reached down and pulled him into the cramped, narrow cabin.

"Are you Major Pitt?"

Pitt looked into the face of a great bull of a man, tan-faced, with long blond sideburns. "Yes, I'm Pitt."

"Welcome back to the roaring twenties, Major. This is some idea, using this old flying fossil for a rescue mission." He held out his hand. "I'm Captain Ben Hull."

Pitt took the massive paw and said, "Best we move out if we expect to beat the snow."

"Right you are," Hull boomed briskly. "No sense in getting ticketed for overparking." If Hull was mildly shocked at Pitt's damaged face, he concealed it well. "We ran this trip without a copilot, a reserved seat in your name, Major. Figured you'd want front row balcony to lead us to the wreck."

Ducking his head to clear the low cockpit door, Pitt moved into the cramped confines and eased his sore body into the worn and cracked leather bucket seat, sitting vacant on the copilot's side. As soon as he was safely strapped in, he turned and found himself staring into the grinning face of Sergeant Sam Cashman.

"Howdy, Major." Cashman's eyes widened. "Who stomped on your face?"

"Tell you some other time." Pitt glanced at the instrument panel, quickly familiarizing himself with the old-fashioned gauges. "I'm a bit surprised to see—"

"To see a sergeant flyin' this mission instead of a genuine flight officer," Cashman finished. "You got no choice, Major. Ah'm the only one on the whole island who's checked out on this old bus. Ain't she a winner? She'll take off and land on a dollar bill and give you change."

"Okay, Sergeant. You're in command. Now let's swing this bird into the wind and get her up. Bear due west along the river until I tell you to cut south."

Cashman merely nodded. Deftly he jockeyed the Tin Goose on a hundred-and-eighty-degree turn until it faced into the wind at the far side of the meadow. Then he shoved the three throttles forward and sent the lumbering old airliner bouncing and shuddering on its way, ever closer to the fence on the opposite end of the field, no more than three hundred feet away.

As they lurched past the front of Golfur Andursson's little house with the plane's tail wheel still glued to the ground, Pitt began to have a vague idea of what Charles Lindbergh's thoughts must have been when he urged his heavily laden Spirit of St. Louis off the muddy runway of Roosevelt Field back in 1927. It seemed impossible to Pitt that any aircraft short of a helicopter or light two-seater could leave the earth in so small a space. He shot a fast look at Cashman and saw only icy calmness and total relaxation. Cashman was indifferently whistling a tune, but Pitt couldn't quite make out the melody above the roar of the trio of two-hundred-horsepower engines.

There was no doubt, Pitt reflected. Cashman certainly displayed the image of a man who knew how to handle a plane, especially this one. With two-thirds of the meadow gone, Cashman eased the control column forward and lifted the tail wheel and then pulled back, floating the plane a few feet above the turf. Then to Pitt's horror, Cashman suddenly dropped the tri-motor back hard on the ground no more than fifty feet in front of the fence. Pitt's horror turned to amazement as Cashman jerked the controls back against his chest and literally bounced the old Tin Goose over the fence and threw it into the air.

"Where did you learn that little trick?" Pitt said, exhaling a great sigh of relief. It was then he recognized the tune Cashman was whistling as the theme from the old movie, "Those Magnificent Men in Their Flying Machines."

"Used to be a crop duster in Oklahoma," Cashman replied.

Pitt couldn't help smiling as he peered through the windshield at the river two hundred feet below. From that height he could easily spot the sloping ridge where Andursson had found him. He saw something now he didn't expect to find. Almost imperceptibly, he became aware of a long even line against the landscape that trailed off toward the south. He pushed open the little side window and looked again. It was there all right: the dark shade of green against the lighter tinted tundra. His foot-prints, where they had sunk into the soft vegetation, had left a path that was easy to follow as the white line down the center of a highway.

Pitt caught Cashman's eye and motioned earth-ward. "To the south. Follow that dark trail to the south."

Cashman banked the plane and stared for a mo-ment out the side window. Then he cocked his head in acknowledgment and turned the nose of the tri-motor southward. Fifteen minutes later he could only wonder at the unerring trail Pitt had made dur-ing his trek to the river. Except for a few occasional deviations around rough or uneven ground, the man-made mark on the earth was almost as straight as a plumb line. Fifteen minutes, that was all the old an-tique needed to cover the same distance that had taken Pitt several hours.

"I have it now," Pit shouted. "There, that crack-like depression where my path ends."

"Where do you want me to set her down, Major?"

"Parallel to the rim of the ravine. There's a flat area running about five hundred feet east and west."

The sky was darkening by the moment—darken-ing with the mist of falling snow. Even as Cashman made his landing approach, the first flakes began dotting the windshield, streaking to the edges of the glass before being blown into the sky by the airstream. Pitt's race had been won, but only by the barest of margins.

Cashman made a safe landing, a smooth landing

considering the rugged terrain and the difficult wind conditions. He timed his run so that the cabin door of the tri-motor ended up within ten yards of the steep drop-off.

The wheels had hardly rolled to a halt when Pitt leaped from the plane and was stumbling, sliding to the bottom of the ravine. Behind him, Hull's men began methodically unloading supplies and arranging them on the dampening ground. Two of the paramedics uncoiled ropes and threw them down the slopes in preparation of bringing up the survivors.

He came upon Lillie still stretched out on his back with Tidi huddled over him. She was talking to Lillie, saying words Pitt couldn't understand, her voice no more than a weak, hoarse whisper; she seemed trying her best to smile, but her lips barely curved in a pitiful grimace.

Pitt knelt down and listened to Lillie's breathing. It was slow and steady. "He'll make it. This guy has guts ten miles long. The big question is whether he'll ever walk again."

Just then Captain Hull approached.

"Take the girl first," Pitt said. "Her ankles are broken."

"My men have set up an aid tent above the slopes. There's a stove warming in it now. She'll be comfortable there until the Icelandic Search and Rescue Team can transport her to Reykjavik." Hull wiped his eyes tiredly. "Their cross-country vehicles are homing in on our radio signals now."

"Can't you airlift her out?"

Hull shook his head. "Sorry, Major. That old tri-motor can only carry eight stretcher cases on one trip. I'm afraid the first load will have to be the most critically injured." He nodded down at Lillie. "How bad is this one?"

"Fractured shoulders and pelvis."

Two of Hull's men appeared carrying an aluminum basket stretcher. "Take the man first," he ordered. "And see that you handle him gently. This one is a back injury."

The paramedics carefully eased Lillie's inert form into the stretcher and attached the ropes for the ascent to the top of the ravine. Pitt couldn't help but be impressed and thankful for the efficiency and smoothness of the lifting lines. Just three minutes later Hull had returned for Tidi.

"Handle her with care, Captain. She happens to be Admiral Sandecker's private secretary."

Kelly was white with snow, lying there vacantly staring at the clouds when Pitt found him. His face, calm and serene, had the expression of a man untouched by pain, a man who was happy and content and at last at peace with himself. A medic was bending over, examining him.

"Heart?" Pitt asked softly, somehow afraid he might wake him.

"Considering his age, that's as safe a bet as any, sir." The medic turned and motioned to Hull, who was standing but a few feet away. "Shall we evacuate him now, Captain?"

"Leave him lay," Hull said. "It's our job to save

the living. As long as there is a chance to keep any one of these people from joining him, our attention must go to them."

"You're right, of course," Pitt said wearily. "This is your show, Captain."

Hull's tone softened. "You know this man, sir?"

"I wish I had known him better. His name is Sam Kelly."

The name obviously meant nothing to Hull. "Why don't you let us take you topside, Major. You're in a pretty bad way yourself."

"No. I'll stay with Sam here." Pitt reached over and gently closed Kelly's eyes for the final time and lightly brushed the snowflakes from the old wrinkled face.

Hull stood unmoving for nearly a minute, groping for words. He started to say something but thought better of it and instead simply nodded his head in silent understanding. Then he turned and plunged back to work.

14

Sandecker closed the file and put it down, then leaned forward as if he were about to spring. "You're asking too much ... too much," he said to the heavyset man sitting across from him.

"I don't enjoy this sort of thing, but time is a commodity we can't afford. This whole scheme, a naive scheme, spawned by Hermit Limited is totally impractical. I admit it sounds inspiring and all that. Save the world, build a paradise. Who knows, maybe F. James Kelly has the answer for the future. But at the moment, he is the leader of a gang of maniacs who have murdered nearly thirty people. And, exactly ten hours from now, he plans to assassinate two heads of state. Our course is determined by one elementary fact—he must be stopped. And Major Pitt is the only one who is physically capable of recognizing Kelly's hired killers."

Sandecker threw the papers on the desk. "Physically capable. Nothing but words that have no feeling." He pushed himself from the chair and began pacing the room. "You're asking me to order a man who has been like a son to me, a man who has been beaten within an inch of death, to get up from a hospital bed and track down a gang of vicious killers six thousand miles from here?" Sandecker shook his head. "You don't know the half of what you're demanding from human flesh and blood. There are limits to a man's courage. Dirk has already done far more than was expected of him."

"Granted that courage is reduced by expenditure. And I agree that the major has done more than was thought humanly possible. There are few if any of my men who could have pulled that rescue off."

"It could be we're arguing over nothing," Sandecker said. "Pitt may not be in any condition to leave the hospital."

"I'm afraid your fears . . . or should I say hopes? . . . are groundless." The bald man checked through a brown folder. "I have here a few observations from my agents, who by the way have been guarding the major." He paused, reading, then went on. He has been stitched, massaged and taped. Fortunately, the only major damage was to his ribs and at that the fractures were minor."

Sandecker's face was cold and blank. He turned as one of the embassy secretaries poked her head around a door.

"Major Pitt is here, sir."

Sandecker glared at the fat man. The fat man shrugged and said nothing.

Sandecker stiffened. His eyes looked resentfully into the fat man's. "Okay, send him in."

Pitt came through the door and shut it behind him. He moved stiffly across the room to a vacant sofa and very slowly eased into the soft cushions. His entire face was swathed in bandages. Only the slits for his eyes and nose plus the top opening for a patch of black hair gave any indication of life beneath the rolls of white gauze. Sandecker tried to look behind the bandages. The deep green eyes that were visible never seemed to flicker.

Sandecker sat down behind the desk and clasped his hands behind his head. "Do the doctors at the hospital know where you are?"

Pitt smiled. "I suspect they'll wonder in another half hour."

"I believe you've met this gentleman." Sandecker motioned to the fat man.

"We've talked over the telephone," Pitt answered. "We haven't been formally introduced . . . at least not with proper names."

The fat man moved quickly around the desk and offered Pitt his hand. "Kippmann, Dean Kippmann."

Pitt took the hand. It was a fooler. There was nothing weak and fat about the grip. "Dean Kippmann," Pitt repeated. "The chief of the National Intelligence Agency. There's nothing like playing with the big leaguers."

"We deeply appreciate your help," Kippmann said warmly. "Do you feel up to a little air travel?"

"After Iceland, a little South American sun couldn't hurt."

"You'll enjoy the sun all right." Kippmann stroked the skin on his head again. "Particularly the southern California variety."

"Southern California?"

"By four o'clock this afternoon."

"By four o'clock this afternoon?"

"Yes, and in fact we've got no time to lose. We've got a plane to catch," Kippmann said as he checked his watch. "I'll fill you in on the way."

Fifteen minutes later, without a further word being spoken, they arrived at the Keflavik Air Field to find an Air Force B-92 reconnaissance bomber waiting by the terminal. Another ten minutes and the supersonic jet was speeding down the runway, soaring out over the ocean.

Sandecker, alone in the terminal, watched the plane lifting into the azure sky, his eyes following it until it disappeared into the distance of the cloudless horizon. Then, wearily, he walked back to the car.

Because of the seven-hour time gain in flying from east to west and the twelve-hundred-mile-per-hour-plus speed of the jet bomber, it was still on the morning of the same day he left Iceland when a bleary-eyed Pitt yawned, stretched in the confined limitations of the tiny cabin, and looking idly out the navigator's side window, watched the tiny shadow of the aircraft dart across the green slopes of the Sierra Madre mountains.

And what now? Pitt smiled wryly back at his reflection in the glass as the bomber now swung out of the foothills and across the smog-blanketed San Gabriel Valley. Gazing down at the Pacific Ocean as it came into view, he cleared his mind of the past and directed it on the immediate future. He didn't know how nor did he have even a remote scrap for a plan, but he knew, no matter the obstacles, he knew he was going to kill Oskar Rondheim.

His mind abruptly returned to the present as the landing gear thumped down and locked into place at the same moment that Dean Kippmann nudged him on the arm.

"Have a nice nap?"

"Slept like the dead."

The B-92 touched down and the engines screamed as the pilot threw the thrust into reverse. The day outside looked warm and comfortable and the California sun gleamed blindingly on the long rows of military jets parked along the taxiways. Pitt read the twelve-foot-high letters painted across a giant hangar: WELCOME TO EL TORO MARINE AIR STATION.

The bomber's engines slowly died and an automobile sped over the apron as Pitt, Kippmann, and the Air Force crew climbed down a narrow ladder to the concrete. Two men unreeled from a blue Ford stationwagon and approached Kippmann. Greetings and handshakes were exchanged. Then they all walked back to the car. Pitt, left standing with nothing to do, followed them.

Beside an open car door the three men huddled together and conversed in undertones while Pitt stood several feet away. Finally Kippmann turned and came over.

"It seems we're about to crash a family reunion."

"Meaning?"

"They're all here. Kelly, Marks, Rondheim, the whole lot."

"Here in California?" Pitt asked incredulously.

"Yes, we had them traced as soon as they left Iceland. The serial number you found on that black jet came home a winner. Hermit Limited purchased six of the same model with consecutive numbers from the factory. We have every one of the remaining five planes under surveillance at this moment."

"I'm impressed. That was fast work."

Kippmann dropped a smile. "Not all that tough. It might have been if the planes had been scattered around the globe, but as it is, they're all sitting neatly side by side exactly eight miles from here at the Orange County Airport."

"Then Kelly's headquarters must be nearby."

"In the hills behind Laguna Beach, a fifty-acre complex," Kippmann said, pointing in a southwesterly direction. "Incidentally, Hermit Limited has over three hundred employees on the payroll who think they're doing classified political analysis for their own government."

"Where do we go from here?"

Kippmann motioned Pitt into the car. "Disneyland," he said solemnly, "to stop a double murder."

They pulled onto the Santa Ana Freeway and

headed north, weaving in and out of the light morning traffic. Kippmann produced two photographs and shoved them in front of Pitt. "Here are the men we're trying to save."

Pitt tapped the face in one of the photos. "This is Pablo Castile, President of the Dominican Republic."

Kippmann nodded. "A brilliant economist and one of the leading members of the Latin American right. Since his inauguration he has begun an ambitious program of reforms. For the first time the people of his country are projecting an atmosphere of confidence and optimism. Our state department would hate to see Kelly mess things up just when there's hope of the Dominican Republic becoming economically stable."

Pitt held up the other photo. "I can't place him."

"Juan De Croix," Kippmann said. "A highly successful doctor of East Indian ancestry. Leader of the People's Progressive Party—won the election only six months ago. Now President of French Guiana."

The car turned off the freeway onto Harbor Boulevard and soon pulled up to the employees' gate of the theme park, and while the driver showed his credentials and asked directions from the guard, Pitt leaned out the window and watched the monorail train pass overhead. They were at the north end of the park and all he could see over the landscaped mounds that surrounded the buildings was the top half of the Matterhorn and the turrets on the Fantasyland castle. The gate was pushed open and they were passed in.

By the time Pitt walked down the underground hallway to the park security offices, he was beginning to think how good that hospital bed in Reykjavik had felt and wondered how soon he could fall into a replacement. He wasn't sure what he expected to find in the park security offices but he had hardly envisioned what he stepped into.

The main conference room was huge; it looked like a scaled-down version of the war room at the Pentagon. The main table ran for at least fifty feet and was circled by over twenty people. There was a radio in one corner and the operator was busily pointing out locations to a marker who stood on a ramp beneath a map that must have stretched ten feet high and covered half the facing wall. Pitt walked slowly around the table and stood under the beautifully contoured and painted map of Disneyland. He was studying the many colored lights and the trail of blue fluorescent tape the marker was laying through the park traffic areas when Kippmann tapped him on the shoulder.

"Major Dirk Pitt, allow me to introduce Mr. Dan Lazard, Chief of Park Security."

Lazard's grip was firm. "Mr. Kippmann has filled me in concerning your injuries. Do you think you're up to this?"

"I can handle it," Pitt said somberly. "But we'll have to do something about my bandaged profile— it's a bit conspicuous."

A glint of amusement came into Lazard's eyes. "I think we can fix it so no one will notice your bandages—not even the nurse who taped them."

Later Pitt stood in front of the full-length mirror and struck a menacing pose as he stared at the life-sized figure of the Big Bad Wolf, who impolitely stared back at him.

"You've got to admit," Kippmann said, fighting back a chuckle, "your own mother wouldn't recognize you in that rig."

"How much time have we left?" Pitt said, fighting back the desire to burst out laughing, in spite of the seriousness of the situation.

"Another hour and forty minutes to go before Kelly's deadline."

"Don't you think I should be sent in the game now? You're not leaving me much time to spot the killers . . . if I can spot them."

"Between my men, the park security staff and agents from the F.B.I., there must be close to forty people concentrating every effort on stopping the assassination. I'm saving you for when we come down to the wire."

"Scraping the bottom of the barrel for a last-ditch attempt." Pitt leaned back and relaxed. "I can't say I agree with your tactics."

"You're not working with amateurs, Major. Every one of those people out there is a pro. Some are dressed in costumes like you, some are walking hand in hand like lovers on a holiday, some are playing the part of families enjoying the rides, others have taken over as attendants. We even have men stationed on roofs and in the dummy second-story offices with telescopes and binoculars." Kippmann's voice was soft, but it carried total conviction. "The killers will be found and stopped before they do their dirty work. The odds we've stacked against Kelly meeting his goal and deadline are staggering."

"Tell that to Oskar Rondheim," Pitt said. "There's the flaw that knocks the hell out of your good intentions—you don't know your adversary."

The silence lay heavy in the small room. Kippmann rubbed his palms across his face, then shook his head slowly, as if he were about to do something he intensely disliked. He picked up the ever-present briefcase and handed Pitt a folder marked simply 078–34.

"Granted, I haven't met him face to face, but he is no stranger to me." Kippmann read from the folder. " 'Oskar Rondheim, alias Max Rolland, alias Hugo von Klausen, alias Chatford Marazan, real name Carzo Butera, born in Brooklyn, New York.' I could go on for hours about his arrests, his convictions. He was pretty big along the New York waterfront. Organized the fishermen's union. Got muscled out by the syndicate and dropped from sight. Over the past few years we kept close tabs on Mr. Rondheim and his albatross industries. We finally put two and two together and came up with Carzo Butera."

Just then the door opened wide. Lazard stood framed in the doorway, his face ashen.

Kippmann stared at him curiously. "Dan, what is it?"

Lazard wiped his brow and slumped into an empty chair. "De Croix and Castile have suddenly changed their planned excursion. They've shaken their escort and disappeared somewhere in the park."

Frowning, baffled, Kippmann's face expressed a moment of utter uncomprehension. "How could that happen? How could you lose them with half the federal agents in the state guarding their party?"

"There are twenty thousand people out there in the park right this minute," Lazard said in a patient tone. "It doesn't take any great feat of cleverness to misplace two of them." He shrugged helplessly. "De Croix and Castile hated our heavy security precautions from the second they stepped through the main gate. They went to the john together and gave us the slip by ducking out a side window, just like a pair of kids."

Pitt stood up. "Quickly, do you have their tour and scheduled stops?"

Lazard stared at him for a moment. "Yes, here, each amusement and exhibit and their time schedules." He handed Pitt a Xeroxed sheet of paper.

Pitt rapidly glanced at the schedule. Then a slow grin cut his face as he turned to Kippmann. "You'd better send me into the game, coach."

Kippmann gave up. "You win. Now where are De Croix and Castile?"

"The obvious." Pitt smiled at Kippmann and Lazard. "The most obvious place where any two men who passed their childhood near the Spanish Main would head."

"You've hit it," Lazard said almost bitterly. "The last stop on the schedule—*The Pirates of the Caribbean*."

* * *

Next to the cleverly engineered apparitions in the Disneyland Haunted House, The Pirates of the Caribbean is the most popular attraction in the world-famous park. Constructed on two underground levels that occupy nearly two acres, the quarter-of-a-mile boat ride carries awed passengers through a maze of tunnels and vast rooms decorated as roving pirate ships and pillaged seaside towns, manned by almost a hundred lifelike figures that not only match the best of Madame Tussaud's, but who also sing, dance, and loot.

Pitt was the last one up the entrance ramp to the landing where attendants assist customers into the boats at the start of the fifteen-minute excursion. The fifty or sixty people waiting in line waved to Pitt and made smiling remarks about his costume as he made his way behind Kippmann and Lazard.

Lazard grasped the managing attendant by the arm. "Quickly, you must stop the boats."

The attendant, a blond, lanky boy no more than twenty years of age, simply stood there in mute uncomprehension.

Lazard, obviously a man who disliked wasted conversation, moved hurriedly across the landing to the controls, disengaged the underwater traction chain that pulled the excursion boats, set the handbrake and turned to face the stunned boy again.

"Two men, two men together, have they taken the ride?"

The dazed boy could only stammer. "I . . . I don't

know for sure, sir. There . . . there's been so many. I can't recall them all—"

Kippmann stepped in front of Lazard and showed the boy the photographs of Castile and De Croix. "Do you recognize these men?"

The boy's eyes widened. "Yes, sir, now I remember." Then a frown spread across his youthful face. "But they weren't alone. There were two other men with them."

"Four!" Kippmann shouted, turning about thirty heads. "Are you sure?"

"Yes, sir." The boy nodded his head violently. "I'm positive. The boat holds eight people. The first four seats held a man and woman with two kids. The men in the photographs took the rear seats with two other men."

Pitt arrived just then, his breath coming in short pants, his hand clutching the handrail as he fought off the pain and exhaustion. "Was one of them a big guy with a bald head, hairy hands? And the other, red-faced with a huge moustache and shoulders like an ape?"

The boy stared dumbly for a moment at Pitt's disguise. Then his expression took on a half smile. "You hit them exactly. A real pair."

"How many boats ago did they board?" Pitt asked the boy.

"Ten, maybe twelve. They should be sitting about halfway, probably somewhere between the burning village and the cannon battle."

"This way!" Lazard almost snapped the words. He

disappeared through a doorway at the end of the landing marked EMPLOYEES ONLY.

As they moved into the blackness that cloaked the mechanical workings of the pirates, the sound of voices from the passengers of the stalled boats could be heard murmuring throughout the cavernous amusement ride. Castile and De Croix, as well as their assassins, Pitt reflected, could have little suspicion as to the delay, but even so, it didn't seem to matter: there was every possibility that Kelly's and Rondheim's scheme had already been carried out. He fought off the ache in his chest and followed the squat, dim form of Kippmann past a story-land setting of five pirates burying a treasure chest. The figures seemed so lifelike it was difficult for Pitt to believe they were only electronically controlled mannequins. He was so engrossed in the simulated reality of the scene that he rammed into Kippmann, who had stopped abruptly.

"Easy, easy," Kippmann protested.

Lazard motioned to them to stay where they were as he moved catlike along a narrow corridor and leaned over the railing of a workman's gallery running over the canal that supported the boats. Then he waved Pitt and Kippmann forward.

"We got lucky for a change," he said. "Take a look."

Pitt, his eyes not yet accustomed to the dark, stared below. There in a boat almost directly under a bridge that ran over the water were Castile and De Croix. And, sitting ominously like disinterested statues on the seat directly in back of the South American Presidents, Pitt could make out the two men who had held his arms while Rondheim had battered him to a pulp only two days before in Reykjavik.

Pitt glanced at the luminous dial of the orange-faced Doxa watch on his wrist. Still an hour and twenty minutes before Kelly's countdown. Too early, far too early, yet there were two of Rondheim's killers sitting not three feet from their intended victims. A very large piece was missing from the puzzle. He had no doubt that Kelly told the truth about his timetable and that Rondheim would stick to it. But would he? If Rondheim meant to take over Hermit Limited, it stood to reason that he just might make a change in plans.

"This is your show, Dan." Kippmann spoke softly to the security director. "How do we take them?"

"Okay," Lazard began. "The bridge will give us enough cover to close within five feet. I'll work around and come out of that doorway under the grogshop sign. Kippmann, you hide behind the mule and wagon."

"Need an extra hand?" Pitt asked.

"Sorry, Major." Lazard gave Pitt a cool stare. "You're hardly in shape for hand-to-hand combat." He paused and gripped Pitt's shoulder. "You could pull off a vital role though."

"Say the word."

"By standing on the bridge in your wolf costume and mingling with the pirates, you could distract those two in the boat long enough to give Kippmann and myself a few more seconds of insurance."

"I guess it's better than matching wits with the three little pigs," Pitt said.

As soon as Lazard found an emergency call box and ordered the attendant to start the canal boats moving in two minutes, he and Kippmann dropped behind the realistic-looking building fronts and took their positions.

Pitt moved to the center of the arched bridge over the canal and joined in the singing amid three merry buccaneers who sat with their legs dangling over the fake stone parapet, swirling their cutlasses around in circles in tune with the songfest. Pitt in his Big Bad Wolf suit and the frolicking pirates presented a strange sight to the people in the boat as they waved and sang a famous old seafaring ditty. The children, a girl about ten and a boy, Pitt guessed, no more than seven, soon recognized him as the three-dimensional cartoon character and began waving back.

Castile and De Croix also laughed and then saluted him in Spanish, pointing and joking to themselves while the tall, bald assassin and his accomplice, the broad-shouldered brute, sat stoney-faced, unmoved by the performance. It occurred to Pitt that he was on thin ice, on which not merely a false move, but the tiniest miscalculation of any detail could spell death to the men, woman and children who sat innocently enjoying his antics.

Then he saw the boat move.

The bow was just passing under his feet when the shadowy figures of Kippmann and Lazard leaped from their cover, sprinted through the mass of animated figures and dropped into the rear of the boat. The surprise was complete.

Pitt had one fleeting glimpse of a flashing metallic glint in the fiery light, and the instinctive slight inclination of his head saved his life as a pirate's cutlass sliced through the crooked top hat that was perched on the wolf mask. Pitt had caught one of Rondheim's men before he knew what was happening, but the other had gained sufficient time to counter Pitt's attack and catch him off balance.

Blindly fending off the lunging thrusts, staggering backward under the fury of the other man's assault, Pitt hurled himself convulsively sideways and over the parapet, and plunged into the cool water of the canal. Even as he dived, Pitt had heard the swish of the pirate's blade as it hissed through the empty air where his body had stood only an instant before. And then there was the sudden shock as his shoulder collided with vicious force against the shallow bottom of the canal. The pain exploded in him and everything seemed to dissolve and stop.

All he could think of was that a killer was somewhere close by, disguised as one of the pirates. He felt helpless, the mannequins all began to look alike, and the action on the bridge had happened with such speed that he hadn't been able to perceive any details of the man's costume.

A second later, he was half running, half stumbling along the quay, gasping at every step as waves of pain shot through every tendon of his body. He burst through a black curtain and into the next stage set. It had a huge domed chamber dimly lit for a nighttime scene.

Built into the far wall, a scaled-down version of a pirate's corsair ship, complete with dummy crew and Jolly Roger rippling in a breeze urged on by a hidden electric fan, fired simulated broadsides from replica cannon across fifty feet of water and over the heads of the people in the excursion boat at a miniature fortress sitting high atop a jagged cliff on the opposite side of the cavernous chamber.

It was too dark to make out any details on the excursion boat. Pitt could detect no movement at the stern and he felt certain that Kippmann and Lazard had everything under their command—everything, that is, that was within their reach. As his eyes began to penetrate the heavy darkness of the simulated nighttime harbor between the ship and the fortress, he saw that the bodies in the boat were all huddled below the sides of the hull.

And then suddenly he was standing in back of a form in a pirate costume who was holding something in his hand and pointing it at the little boat in the water. Pitt raised the cutlass and brought the flat side of the blade down on the pirate's wrist.

The pirate swung around, the white hair falling from under a scarlet bandanna that was knotted around his head, the cold blue-gray eyes flashing with anger and frustration, the lines about the mouth deeply etched. His voice was hard and metallic.

"It seems I am your prisoner."

Pitt wasn't fooled for an instant. The man behind the voice was dangerous and he was playing for high stakes. But Pitt had more than an edged weapon—he had a newly found strength that was suddenly coursing through his body like a gathering tidal wave. He began to smile.

"Ah—so it is you, Oskar."

Pitt paused significantly, watching Rondheim like a cat. Holding Hermit Limited's chief executioner on the end of the cutlass, Pitt pulled off the rubber wolf's head. Rondheim's face was still set and hard, but the eyes betrayed total incomprehension. Pitt dropped the mask, bracing himself for the moment he had planned for but never really believed would happen. Slowly, he unwrapped the bandages with one hand, letting the gauze fall to the deck in little unraveled piles, building the suspense. When he finished, he gazed steadily at Rondheim and stood back. Rondheim's lips began to work in a half-formed question and a dazed expression spread across his features.

"Sorry you can't recall the face, Oskar," Pitt said quietly. "But you didn't leave a great deal to recognize."

Rondheim stared at the swollen eyes, the bruised and puffed lips, the sutures that laced the cheekbones and eyebrows, and then his mouth fell open and in a whisper he breathed, "Pitt!"

Pitt laughed. "I apologize for ruining your day, but it just goes to prove that you can't always trust a computer."

Rondheim looked at Pitt long and searchingly. "And the others?"

"With one exception, they're all alive and mending the broken bones you so generously dispensed." Pitt focused his gaze beyond Rondheim's shoulder and saw that the excursion boat was safely entering the next gallery.

"Then it's back to you and me again, Major. Under conditions more favorable to you than those I enjoyed in the gym. But don't get your hopes up."

"I admit I misled you, Oskar. Round one was an unequal contest. You had the numbers, the planning and the initiative from the beginning. How are you alone, Oskar, without your paid help to prop your victims? How are you when you're on strange ground? You still have time to escape. Nothing stands between you and a chance for freedom except me. But there's the rub, Oskar. You have to get by me."

An uncertain smile came to Rondheim's mouth as he crouched in a karate stance. The smile didn't last. Pitt hit him. He hit Rondheim with a right cross, a perfectly timed punch that jerked Rondheim's head sideways and staggered him into the ship's main mast.

Deep down Pitt had known that he had little chance of taking Rondheim in a prolonged fight, that he couldn't hold the other man off for more than a few minutes, but he had schemed and timed for the element of surprise, the one advantage that played on his side before the karate blows could lash his face again. As it turned out, the advantage was a small one.

Rondheim was incredibly tough; he had taken a hard blow, yet he was already recovering. He sprang from the mast and threw a kick to Pitt's head, missing by a scant inch as Pitt ducked easily away. The ill timing cost him. Pitt caught Rondheim with a series of left jabs and another short, hard right that sent him to his knees on the deck, holding a hand to a broken, bleeding nose.

"You've improved," Rondheim whispered through the streaming blood.

"I said I misled you." Pitt was hanging back tensed in a half boxing, half judo position, waiting for Rondheim's next move. "You were an easy man to lead astray, Oskar, or should I call you by the name on your birth certificate? No matter, your run has played out."

Mouthing a string of curses through blood-specked lips, his face now frozen in insane hate, Rondheim flung himself at Pitt. He hadn't taken a second step when Pitt brought an uppercut from the deck and rammed it as solidly as a sledgehammer into Rondheim's teeth. Pitt had given it everything he had, thrown his shoulder and body into it with such force that his ribs screamed in agony and he knew even as he did it that he could never marshal the strength to do it again.

He stepped over the sprawling legs of the unconscious man and bent down, propping one of Rondheim's arms against the deck and the bottom base of the railing. Rondheim stirred sluggishly and moaned.

With a feeling of emptiness, almost sadness, Pitt sat there and stared down at the limp figure of Rondheim. He was sitting there like that when Kippmann and Lazard came charging across the deck, followed by a small army of security men.

"It's Rondheim," Pitt said vaguely.

"Rondheim? Are you sure?"

"I seldom forget a face," Pitt said.

Lazard turned to look at him. His lips twisted in a wry smile. "What was it I said about you hardly being in shape for hand-to-hand combat?"

"What happens to Kelly and Hermit Limited?" Pitt asked, seeming to ignore the question.

"We'll arrest Mr. Kelly along with his internationally wealthy partners, of course, but the chances of convicting men of their stature are almost impossible. I should imagine the governments involved will hurt them where it hurts them most—in the pocketbook. The fines they'll probably have to pay should build the Navy a new aircraft carrier."

Kippmann nodded to Pitt. "We have you to thank, Major Pitt, for blowing the whistle on Hermit Limited."

Lazard smiled suddenly. "And I'd like to be the first to express my gratitude for your Horatius-at-the-bridge act. Kippmann and I couldn't be standing here now if you hadn't taken the cue when you did." He put his hand on Pitt's shoulder. "Tell me something. I'm curious."

"About what?"

"How did you know those pirates on the bridge were real flesh and blood?"

"As the man once said," Pitt said casually, "there we were just sitting on the bridge, eyeball to eyeball . . . and I could swear I saw the other guys blink."

Epilogue

It was a pleasant Southern California evening. The day's smog had cleared away and a cool breeze from the west carried the strong, clean smell of the Pacific Ocean through the center garden of the Disneyland Hotel, soothing the soreness of Pitt's injuries and tranquilizing his mind for the task ahead. He stood silent, waiting for the glass-enclosed elevator to descend along the exterior of the building.

The elevator hummed and stopped and the doors slid open. He entered and pushed the button marked six. The elevator rose swiftly, and he turned and looked through the windows at the skyline of Orange County. He took a deep breath and slowly exhaled, watching the sparkling carpet of lights spread and widen toward the dark horizon as the first three floors slid by. The lights blinked in the crystal air, reminding him of a jewel box.

It hardly seemed like two hours since the park doctor had set his wrist and Pitt had showered and shaved and eaten his first solid meal since leaving

Reykjavik. The doctor was quite definite that he go to a hospital, but Pitt wouldn't hear of it.

The elevator slowed and stopped, the door opened and Pitt stepped onto the soft red carpet of the sixth-floor foyer. He abruptly halted in midstep to keep from colliding with three men who were waiting to go down. Two of the men he took to be Kippmann's agents. Of the third man, the one slumped head downward in the middle, there was no doubt, it was F. James Kelly.

Pitt stood there blocking their way. Kelly slowly lifted his head and stared at Pitt vacantly, unrecognizing. Finally Pitt broke the uneasy silence.

"I'm almost sorry your grand scheme failed, Kelly. In theory, it was glorious. In execution, it was impossible."

Kelly's eyes widened by slow degrees and the color drained from his face. "Is that you, Major Pitt? But no . . . you're . . ."

"Supposed to be dead?" Pitt finished, as if it no longer mattered too much except to himself.

"Oskar swore he killed you."

"I managed to leave the party early," Pitt said coldly.

Kelly shook his head back and forth. "Now I understand why my plan failed. It seems, Major, that fate cast you in the role of my avenging nemesis."

"Purely a matter of my being at the wrong place at the wrong time."

Kelly smiled thinly and nodded to the two agents. The three of them entered the waiting elevator.

Pitt stood aside, then suddenly said, "Sam left you a message."

Kelly took seconds to recover. "Is Sam—"

"Sam died out on the tundra," Pitt finished. "Near the end he wanted you to know he forgave you."

"Oh, no . . . oh, no," Kelly moaned, his fingers covering his eyes.

For many years afterward, Pitt carried the mental picture of Kelly's face just before the elevator door closed. The stricken lines, the dull, lifeless eyes, the ashen skin. It was the face of a man who looked as if he was strangling.

Pitt tried the door with the numerals 605. It was locked. He walked down the hall and turned the doorknob to Room 607. It opened. He quietly stepped over the threshold and eased the door closed. The room was cool and dark. The smell of stale cigar butts invaded his nostrils before he passed through the entry hall. The odor was all he needed to know it was Rondheim's room.

Moonlight filtered through the drapes, casting long shapeless shadows as he searched through the bedroom, noting that Rondheim's clothes and luggage were undisturbed. Kippmann had kept his word. His men had been careful not to alert Kirsti Fyrie or give her the slightest warning of Rondheim's fate or the sudden demise of Hermit Limited.

He moved toward a shaft of yellow light that split the half-open door to the adjoining room. He entered, treading softly, noiselessly like a night animal ready to spring. It could hardly be called a room, a plush suite would have been a fairer description. It consisted of a hall, a living room, a bathroom and a bedroom, edged on one side by a large sliding glass door that led to a small balcony.

Kirsti walked through the bedroom into the living room and saw Pitt's reflection in the window. She clutched the edge of the couch, silent, her eyes searching him. "Dirk!" she whispered softly. "It's you. It's really you. Thank goodness you're still alive."

"Your concern for my welfare comes a little late."

"I had to do what I've done," she said faintly. "But I swear to you I have killed no one. I was unwillingly pulled into the vortex by Oskar. I never dreamed that his association with Kelly would lead to death for so many."

An awkward silence descended. Finally Kirsti stared at Pitt and said, "There is a price; there always has to be a price."

"It's cheap enough considering your past mistakes . . . mistakes you can never buy back even with your fortune. But you can clean the slate and make a new life without outside intrusion. All I want is your guarantee for close and continued cooperation between Fyrie Limited and NUMA."

"And?"

"The memory banks in Kelly's computers contain enough data to build a new undersea probe. I speak for Admiral Sandecker when I say he would like you to head up the project."

"That's all, nothing more?" she asked incredulously.

"I said the price was cheap."

She gazed levelly at him. "Tomorrow, next week, the coming year, how can I be sure you will not decide to raise the interest rate?"

Pitt's eyes turned cold and his voice was like ice. "Don't put me in the same league with your other playmates. Murder and extortion have never turned me on."

She hesitated. "I'm sorry, truly sorry. What else can I say."

He didn't answer, just looked at her.

She turned and gazed out the window at the park.

"And where do you go from here?" she asked.

"After a short vacation, I'll go back to NUMA headquarters in Washington and begin work on a new project."

She turned to look at him. "And if I asked you to come to Iceland with me and become a member of my board of directors?"

"I'm not the board-of-director type."

They stood in the center of the room, facing each other silently. Pitt's features were coldly menacing. The purplish bruises, the swollen flesh, the jagged cuts all worked together in one terrible mask of disgust. He could only see the unidentifiable ashes of what had once been men. He saw Hunnewell dying on a lonely beach. He remembered the face of the captain of the hydroplane before he disappeared in flames. He knew the pain of Lillie, Tidi, and Sam Kelly. And he knew Kirsti Fyrie was partly responsible for their suffering and for some—their deaths.

Kirsti paled and backed away a step. "Dirk, what's the matter?"

"God save thee," he said.

He turned and opened the door. The first few steps toward the elevator were the hardest. Then it got easier. By the time he reached the main floor, walked to the curb and hailed a cab, the old confident, relaxed composure was back.

The driver opened the door and dropped the flag.

"Where to, sir?"

Pitt sat there a moment in silence. Then suddenly he knew where he had to go. He had to pick up where he left off when Sandecker had called him for this job.

"The Newporter Inn. I have a lot of relaxing to catch up on."

About the Author

Clive Cussler's life nearly parallels that of his hero, Dirk Pitt®. Whether searching for lost aircraft or leading expeditions to find famous shipwrecks, he has had amazing success. With his NUMA crew of volunteers, Cussler has discovered more than sixty lost ships of historic importance, including the long-lost Confederate submarine *Hunley*. Like Pitt, Cussler collects classic automobiles. His collection features eighty examples of custom coachwork and is one of the finest to be found anywhere. Cussler divides his time between the deserts of Arizona and the mountains of Colorado.